SECOND CHANCE

"Kristin?" Mr. Thompson was waiting for her in the living room. The mantel clock was just chiming the half hour: ten-thirty.

"Dad, look, I'm so sorry—"

"I've been worried sick," Mr. Thompson cut her off. "You promised me you'd be back in an hour, and then you show up three hours late."

Kristin took a deep breath. "We ended up going somewhere different than—"

"I'm disappointed in you, Kristin," Mr. Thompson interrupted again. "I didn't think I needed to say this, but maybe I do. I've watched you work for years and years for the opportunity to join the pro circuit. Now I'm seeing you throw it all away. You aren't even bothering to take care of yourself before the biggest tournament of your life. Doesn't this tournament matter to you anymore?"

Kristin felt as if she had been slapped. She couldn't answer.

"That's all I have to say to you. Now, I'm going to bed," Mr. Thompson said heavily. "And I suggest that you do the same."

Kristin didn't say a word. She just stared at his back as he walked out of the room. If only she could explain that the tournament did matter to her—more than anything in the whole world—but that she also wanted to see what it felt like to be a normal teenager.

Bantam Books in the Sweet Valley High Series
Ask your bookseller for the books you have missed

SWEET VALLEY HIGH

SECOND CHANCE

Written by
Kate William

Created by
FRANCINE PASCAL

BANTAM BOOKS
TORONTO · NEW YORK · LONDON · SYDNEY · AUCKLAND

RL 6, IL age 12 and up

SECOND CHANCE
A Bantam Book / March 1989

Sweet Valley High is a registered trademark of Francine Pascal.

Conceived by Francine Pascal.

Produced by Daniel Weiss Associates, Inc.,
27 West 20th Street, New York, NY 10011

Cover art by James Mathewuse

ISBN 0-553-27771-5

Published simultaneously in the United States and Canada

Bantam Books are published by Bantam Books, a division of Bantam Doubleday
Dell Publishing Group, Inc. Its trademark, consisting of the words "Bantam
Books" and the portrayal of a rooster, is Registered in U.S. Patent and Trademark
Office and in other countries. Marca Registrada. Bantam Books, 666 Fifth Avenue,
New York, New York 10103.

PRINTED IN THE UNITED STATES OF AMERICA

O   0 9 8 7 6 5 4 3 2 1

SECOND CHANCE

One

"Elizabeth Wakefield!" Enid cried, hurrying across the crowded lunchroom with her arms full of file folders and notebooks. Her green eyes sparkled as she plopped down in the seat across from her best friend. "I just finished talking to Mr. Collins. We're ready to start the new chapter of the Sweet Valley High Big Sister–Little Sister program!"

Elizabeth looked eagerly at the material Enid set down on the table. They had been working closely with Roger Collins, their English teacher and faculty adviser, for the past week, trying to get the approval of the National Foundation of

Big Sisters. The foundation matched up little girls who had lost their mothers with high-school girls willing to volunteer their time as "big sisters."

"The foundation sent us a pile of information," Enid said excitedly as she riffled through the files. "They're really thrilled we're going to be starting up this new chapter. And it looks like there're lots of little girls in the area who want to take part in the program."

Elizabeth pushed her tray aside and peered at the list Enid was examining. "Do you think we'll have enough big sisters for all these girls?"

"I sure do," Enid said with confidence. "We've got almost enough now, and I can't imagine anyone not wanting to help out. When you read the stories about these little girls, Liz, it's just heartbreaking. Imagine if you had lost your mother at an early age." Enid shuddered at the thought before continuing. "The foundation says that for some of these girls it makes all the difference in the world having someone older who cares about them, who takes an interest in what they're doing."

"Well, I certainly think it's a fabulous way to help," Elizabeth declared. "And you deserve all the credit, Enid. It was your idea."

Enid blushed. She was a sweet, earnest girl who didn't find it easy to be complimented.

"Oh, come on, Liz," she murmured, pretending to concentrate on the list.

Elizabeth looked at her fondly. She couldn't imagine anyone else devoting so many hours to helping others—and looking embarrassed if someone so much as mentioned it.

Elizabeth and Enid had been best friends for many years. And even though Elizabeth now spent a lot of time with Jeffrey French, her boyfriend, she still felt there were things only she and Enid could share. Not even Elizabeth's twin sister, Jessica, always understood her feelings. Certainly Jessica didn't see anything to like about Enid—"boring Enid," as she liked to say.

Elizabeth and Jessica were identical twins: five feet six inches tall, with willowy figures, shoulder-length blond hair, and eyes the blue-green of the Pacific Ocean. Although they looked alike, the twins were vastly different.

Jessica's motto was to have fun. She sought out change and excitement and loved being the center of attention. As co-captain of the cheerleading squad and a member of Pi Beta Alpha, an exclusive sorority at Sweet Valley High, Jessica was one of the most popular juniors. She loved to shop and always wore the latest fashions. Before she had met A. J. Morgan, her boyfriend, her love life had been as changeable as her wardrobe. It was hard to believe that Jessica had stayed with A.J. for a couple of months. Lately, though, Jessica and A.J. had been arguing. Maybe another change was coming.

Elizabeth, on the other hand, was more serious and industrious. Her dream was to be a writer, and she worked hard at writing for *The Oracle*, the school's newspaper. Mr. Collins, who supervised the paper's staff, knew how dedicated Elizabeth was. He had been only too eager to help Elizabeth and Enid when they explained that they wanted to start a Big Sister chapter at Sweet Valley High.

"Do you think Jessica will want to be a big sister?" Enid asked, startling Elizabeth from her thoughts. "We have a girl here who sounds like the perfect match." She giggled. "Her hobbies are shopping, reading fashion magazines, and boys. When she grows up, she either wants to be a game show hostess or the President."

Elizabeth started to laugh. "You're making that up," she cried, snatching the application form out of Enid's hand. But Enid was telling the truth. Little Allison Post sounded like a real handful. "Maybe Jessica will do it," Elizabeth said thoughtfully.

"Do what?" a deep voice inquired.

Enid and Elizabeth spun around just as Jeffrey slid his tray next to Elizabeth's and squeezed her shoulder affectionately. "Can I join you, or are you having a power lunch here?" Jeffrey asked with a smile.

"We're just looking through the names of little girls the Big Sister program sent us," Elizabeth explained.

Jeffrey looked over her shoulder with interest. "Looks like they sent you quite a few," he said. "How many volunteers have you signed up so far?"

Enid shuffled through some papers. "Actually, we're doing all right," Enid said. "We've signed up nine big sisters, and the chapter has sent us eleven names. Maybe we really *should* try to draft your sister," she added to Elizabeth.

Jeffrey grinned. "Jessica? You mean the same Jessica I just overheard telling A.J. that she wants to spend every spare minute perfecting her tan?"

"I'm sure Jessica will be happy to help out," Elizabeth said half-convincingly. The twins had different personalities and interests, but they loved each other deeply and usually stood up for each other.

"Speaking of the devil," Jeffrey said as Jessica came racing into the cafeteria, her blond hair flying.

"Lizzie," Jessica gasped, hurrying over to the table, "can I have the keys to the Fiat? I have cheerleading practice after school, and then I have *so* many errands to run."

Elizabeth laughed. The twins shared a red Fiat Spider that used to belong to their mother, but sometimes *share* didn't seem like the right word. "How am I going to get home if I give you the keys?" Elizabeth asked sensibly.

Jeffrey patted her on the arm. "I'll bail you out," he promised.

Jessica flashed him a grateful smile. "Thanks," she said, scooping up the keys her sister dangled in front of her.

"Wait a sec, Jess. These come with strings attached," Elizabeth warned. "Enid and I have a favor to ask you."

"That's right, Jess," Enid chimed in. "We've found a little girl in the Big Sister-Little Sister program who we think is just perfect for you. Will you sign up to be her big sister?"

Jessica narrowed her eyes. "Isn't it going to take up a lot of time? I'm incredibly busy for the next few weeks. There's cheerleading, and Pi Beta Alpha, and A.J.—and besides, I want to spend a lot of time on the beach." She frowned as she examined her arms. "Bruce Patman's parents are having one of their enormous parties at the end of the month, and I've got to work on my tan."

Elizabeth groaned. Bruce Patman, the wealthiest boy in the whole school, was as conceited as he was good-looking. The prospect of a party at his parents' country club seemed like a slim excuse for not participating in the Big Sister program. "We're not asking for a huge time commitment. You'd only have to get together with your little sister once a week," Elizabeth said. "Just let us read you a little bit about this girl." She gave Enid a wink as she read Allison's application form out loud.

"She sounds like fun," Jessica admitted. "OK," she added, relenting. "I'll do it. As long as you think it won't take up all my beach time." She pulled the application form over to study it herself. "Allison sounds like a good kid. A.J. and I could probably take her to the beach with us."

Elizabeth wrote her sister's name down next to Allison's with a big flourish. "Thanks, Jess," she said with a big smile as her twin ran off. "You see?" she added to Enid and Jeffrey, who were both laughing. "I told you she'd do it."

"Poor Allison Post," Enid said mirthfully, opening up the next file folder. "She's not going to know what hit her when she meets your sister."

For the next half hour the three of them worked their way through the list of applicants. They paired Jade Wu up with a girl who wanted to be a dancer, they found someone for Lynne Henry, Maria Santelli, Olivia Davidson, DeeDee

Gordon, Cara Walker, and Caroline Pearce, and, of course, Elizabeth and Enid each selected a girl to sponsor.

"How are we doing?" Elizabeth asked when the list of potential sponsors was depleted.

Enid frowned. "We have one girl left, nine-year-old Emily Brown. Her mother was killed last year in a car crash. Her third-grade teacher describes her schoolwork as uneven. She goes on to say, 'Emily needs special attention. She has had a very hard time adjusting to life without her mother. Her biggest interest is tennis. She practices frequently and talks about it constantly. This is a girl who would greatly benefit from the program.'"

"That's really sad," Jeffrey said compassionately.

Elizabeth was frowning. "Who'd be good for her?" she mused. "Do we know anyone who's really into tennis?"

"Bruce Patman," Enid said with a giggle. Bruce, who was one of the best players at Sweet Valley High, loved to brag about his game.

Jeffrey looked thoughtfully at Elizabeth. "What about Kristin Thompson?" he said slowly.

Elizabeth's eyes brightened. "Jeffrey, what a wonderful idea!" she exclaimed.

"Wait a minute," Enid objected. "You two can't honestly think Kristin's going to participate in the Big Sister program. She never even takes a break from practicing tennis!"

All three were quiet for a minute, thinking it over.

Elizabeth barely knew Kristin. Very few people were close to Kristin because she was so dedicated to tennis that she didn't have time for anything—or anyone—else. But people who knew her were aware that Kristin was already a high-caliber tennis player who wanted to be on the pro circuit.

"Kristin's in my math class," Enid volunteered. "I've talked to her a couple of times—you know, about assignments and stuff. She's probably a very nice person, but there's an aloof quality about her. She seems so bent on succeeding that she refuses to be friendly. I think if she had friends it would mean too much time away from tennis."

"I don't think she's unfriendly," Elizabeth objected. "I've seen Kristin practicing out on the courts, and I know she's super-determined. Jeffrey, remember when we invited her to the beach recently on that incredibly hot day? She was really nice, but she wouldn't come because she had a tennis lesson. Kristin's whole life is tennis. That's why she doesn't have time for a lot of other things. But I still think it's worth a try."

"That may be true," Enid said. "I just didn't

want to put her on the spot by asking her to do something she might not be able to do."

"Well, it can't hurt, can it?" Elizabeth asked reasonably. "The very worst that can happen is Kristin will say she's too busy. Then we can find someone else." She glanced down at Emily Brown's application. "I just can't imagine a better match, though. Kristin could probably do this little girl a world of good."

Enid laughed. "You know what I love about you, Elizabeth Wakefield? You always manage to make things seem perfectly simple." Enid's eyes twinkled. "And you're right. Why not ask Kristin? It's not like we're going to force her or anything. And who knows? Maybe this is exactly the sort of thing Kristin would love to do."

Jeffrey nodded. "Being under intense pressure all the time must be hard. I bet Kristin would love a chance to do something completely different for a change."

"That settles it!" Elizabeth cried. "I'm going to find Kristin after school today and see if she wants to be Emily Brown's big sister!"

Two

Kristin Thompson was sitting alone in the library, frowning at the blank notebook in front of her. She glanced at her watch anxiously. At twenty-five minutes past twelve, lunch hour was almost half over, and she still hadn't begun her English paper, "The American Dream," and how it was reflected in the novels they had read that term, was the subject of the essay. It wasn't due for a little over two weeks, but Kristin knew the essay was going to take a lot of work, and with her tennis schedule, she wouldn't have enough time to devote to the paper unless she started early.

"Many of the novels we've read reflect the theme of the American dream," Kristin wrote. A minute later she sighed heavily, balled up the piece of paper, and threw it in the trash can next to her.

The library door opened, and Shelley Novak, a junior on the basketball team, came in, her arms full of books. When the door opened, Kristin could hear the sound of laughter and people talking in the hallway. Kristin suddenly wished she had friends with whom she could enjoy a few laughs. She couldn't remember the last time she had spent an idle lunch hour talking with her classmates.

But time was too valuable. Kristin always ate quickly, then hurried to the library to work. If she spent lunch hour socializing, it would mean an hour lost in practice after school.

And Kristin knew she couldn't stray from her rigorous schedule if she was going to make it as a pro. She was up every morning at six to jog and lift weights or run sprints. And then the minute school got out she sped back on her bike to the tennis club her father owned to practice with Dorrie Graham, her private coach, until dinner. Usually Dorrie joined Kristin and her father for dinner, either at the club or at the Thompsons' home. Kristin didn't even get around to starting her homework until eight-thirty or nine, and she had to be in bed by ten-thirty at the latest. Not exactly a schedule that left a lot of time for having fun.

Shelley came over to Kristin's table to look something up in the unabridged dictionary. "Looks like we're the only two in here," she said, smiling at Kristin. "Do you have a lot of extra homework to catch up on, too?"

"I'm trying to get a head start on an English composition I was assigned this morning," Kristin said, looking ruefully down at her blank notebook. At this rate "The American Dream" wouldn't be finished for about a year!

Shelley found the definition she was looking for in the dictionary and made a note of it. She regarded Kristin with interest. "You're Kristin Thompson, right? The tennis champ?"

Kristin blushed a little. "That's me," she said simply.

"I'm Shelley. Shelley Novak. I'm on the girls' basketball team. I'm a sports fanatic, and I'm always reading about you in the sports pages."

Kristin nodded, feeling shy. She never knew exactly what to say when her classmates commented on her celebrity status. "There's been a lot of coverage now that the Avery Cup tournament is coming up," she said.

Shelley looked intrigued. "I guess that's an important tournament for you."

"It's a very important tournament to me," Kristin said, taking a deep breath. She could feel the adrenaline coursing through her just from talking about the Avery Cup. "There's an all-star team run by a coach named Nick Wylie that gets handpicked from this tournament. If I qualify and win, I'll be on Wylie's team. That'll mean traveling around the world and competing on the pro circuit." Her eyes shone. "It's what I've been working for my whole life."

Shelley looked at her with admiration. "Boy, I hope you win," she said. "Do you feel like you're under a lot of pressure?"

"Well, sort of," Kristin admitted, feeling shy again. "Only I guess that's the way it always is with a serious sport. It must be the same with basketball," she added.

"Well, it's a little different, because I don't want to be a pro basketball player." Shelley shook her head. "I don't think I could handle all the pressure. But I really admire you, Kristin. I'll be rooting for you to win the tournament."

"Thanks," Kristin said, looking down at her notebook. She had always said that tennis was her *whole* life, but she couldn't pretend that she never had any regrets. Sometimes she felt she would give anything in the world not to be under so much pressure, to be like everybody else.

Elizabeth hurried across the front lawn of Sweet Valley High after school that afternoon. She had spotted Kristin Thompson unlocking her royal-blue ten-speed bicycle.

"Kristin!" she called.

The girl looked up in surprise. Elizabeth had forgotten how pretty Kristin was, with her short auburn hair and wide-set hazel eyes. She was dressed in gray sweatpants and a white T-shirt that showed off her deep tan.

"Can I talk to you for a sec?" Elizabeth asked, giving her a friendly smile.

Kristin smiled back. "Oh, hi, Liz. I haven't seen you in a couple of weeks." She glanced at her watch. "I've only got a minute. I have to meet my coach at practice in about fifteen minutes."

Elizabeth took a deep breath. "I know how busy you are, Kristin. And I don't want to put you on the spot by asking you to do something you can't possibly have time for. But my friend Enid Rollins and I are starting up a chapter of the Big Sister program at Sweet Valley High, and we have a little girl with no one to sponsor her. She happens to be a tennis freak, and we wondered. . . ." Elizabeth's voice trailed off.

"What's the Big Sister program?" Kristin asked.

Elizabeth explained to Kristin how the program worked. "It's for little girls—in this case, mostly nine- and ten-year-olds—whose mothers have either left the family or who have passed away. The program tries to help these girls by providing them with an older surrogate sister who can do some of the things for them that their mother might have."

"That's a nice idea," Kristin said slowly, not meeting Elizabeth's gaze.

"Emily Brown is the girl we hoped you might sponsor. She's in third grade. Her mom died in a car crash last year. The only thing she seems to care about right now is tennis. Her teacher thinks she'd really benefit from spending time with an older girl."

Kristin bent over to fuss with her lock. "I'm really incredibly busy right now," she said, not looking at Elizabeth. "The Avery Cup tournament is coming up. I've been practicing four hours a day. I really don't think—"

Elizabeth cleared her throat. "We wouldn't need much of a time commitment. Maybe an hour or two a week. And you don't have to let us know right away. Think about it if you want," she said quickly.

Kristin sighed deeply. "OK," she said abruptly, climbing onto her bike. "I'll think about it."

Before Elizabeth could say another word, Kristin had ridden away.

Kristin blinked back tears. The road swam before her in a blur of colors, and a car slammed on its horn as she rode too close to traffic. She had to breathe deeply to get back her control.

She wished Elizabeth Wakefield hadn't told her about Emily Brown. No one at school was close enough to Kristin to know that her own mother had been killed in a plane crash when she was only seven.

Kristin blinked furiously, trying as hard as she could to shut out the memory of that horrible day, nine years ago now, when she had come home and found her father and Dorrie sitting in the living room, staring blankly at each other. "I can't tell her," her father had said, tears running down his face. "Tell me what?" Kristin had cried.

It was as though part of her life had ended then—the part that had been filled with love, laughter, and happiness. After that there was only one thing that mattered: winning tennis matches.

Kristin rode her bike up the long drive to the tennis club and slipped it into the rack. Hundreds of stormy thoughts raced around in her head. Why had Elizabeth brought up this Big Sister program now, of all times? She'd had everything under perfect control.

"Kristin!" Dorrie called, waving from the courts.

Kristin sighed and went into the clubhouse to change and get her racket. She knew her routine so well that she moved like an automaton, making small talk with the men in the clubhouse, changing in the locker room, limbering up, then running out to the courts, where Dorrie was waiting for her.

Dorrie, who had been her mother's best friend and had played doubles with her on the pro team the year before the tragic crash, had remained her father's closest friend. She had singlehandedly coached Kristin for the past eight years, and sometimes Kristin thought Dorrie knew her even better than she knew herself.

"You seem sluggish. What time did you get to bed last night?" Dorrie called, after they had hit a few balls.

Kristin bit her lip. "Same time as always," she said, taking a deep breath to get her concentration back.

But her serve went into the net.

"Sorry," she called, red-faced, running forward to retrieve the ball.

Dorrie looked at her with concern.

The next serve was perfect—clean, hard, powerful.

"That's my girl!" Dorrie cried. "Let's do it again."

For the next hour Kristin fired serves at Dorrie. On good days her serves were as dependable as the rest of her game. Reporters always wrote that she seemed like a born tennis player. They referred to her balanced game and called her "a sure thing." But this afternoon Kristin felt awkward and heavy on her feet. Nothing seemed to be going right.

"Let's take a break," Dorrie suggested at five-thirty. She strolled over to join Kristin on her side of the net. At thirty-eight, Dorrie was a strikingly attractive woman. Her black hair was slightly streaked with gray, and her bright blue eyes sparkled when she smiled.

"I don't know what's wrong with me today," Kristin muttered before Dorrie could say a word. "I'm playing like a total klutz."

"Everyone's entitled to an off day once in a while," Dorrie said, putting an arm affectionately around Kristin. "Don't worry about it."

But Kristin always worried about her game. "The Avery Cup's so close," she said in anguish. "If I keep playing like this, I'll never make it."

Dorrie kept her voice light. "Remember," she

said, "part of being a pro is learning to live with the ups *and* downs. It's only one afternoon, Kristin. Just relax and you'll be fine."

Kristin didn't answer. She kept thinking about Elizabeth, the Big Sister program, and little Emily Brown. She couldn't get the image of the lonely little girl out of her mind.

Kristin didn't know what Emily Brown looked like, though. The little girl Kristin imagined was really herself, nine years ago, the day she had found out about her mother's accident.

She knew that was why her game was off today, but she would never tell Dorrie that. Kristin had made it a rule never to show her father, or Dorrie, when she was feeling vulnerable and weak. Kristin tried hard to act like a pro on the court and off. That meant being tough—disciplined, as Dorrie said.

A pro doesn't break down and cry just because she gets lonesome sometimes, Kristin reminded herself sternly. She steeled herself and said, "Let's keep going. I'm not leaving the court till I get my serve back!"

Dorrie gave her the thumbs-up sign. "Way to go, champ!" she said enthusiastically. "That's the kind of spirit I've always admired in you, Kristin!"

Kristin bit her lip as she squared off to face the net. That was what she wanted, wasn't it?

For Dorrie and her father to admire her for being strong?

She knew it was. But right then Kristin wasn't feeling one bit strong. It was almost as if the lonely little girl had never grown up at all.

Three

After practice Kristin and Dorrie met Kristin's father in the club's dining hall. They often ate there during the week, since tennis absorbed too much of their time for them to cook. Besides, the club's dining room was practically home to them all. Mr. Thompson owned several tennis clubs and was a partner in a tennis camp outside of San Diego. It kept him busy, and—as he liked to tell people—it kept him close to his daughter.

"Hi, sweetheart!" Neil Thompson called when she came into the dining room, fresh from her shower in the locker room. Her father and Dorrie were sitting at their regular table near the window.

"Hi, Dad," Kristin said, giving him a kiss and sliding into the chair between them. She didn't bother to look at the menu, which she had long ago memorized. "I'd just like some grilled chicken and a salad with no dressing," she told the waiter. Kristin was trying to keep her weight low before the tournament.

"Are you sure that's enough food for you? What about some vegetables? They're not fattening," her father suggested.

Kristin shook her head. "No, thanks. Chicken and salad are just fine."

Mr. Thompson looked at her closely. "Are you feeling all right, sweetheart? Dorrie was just telling me your game was a little shaky this afternoon."

Kristin took a big swallow of water. "I'm fine," she said in a low voice. She knew her father's questions only came out of love, but sometimes she wished he wouldn't pay such close attention to her.

"I've heard there's a flu going around," he added anxiously.

"Dad, I'm fine!" Kristin exclaimed.

Dorrie put her hand restrainingly on Mr. Thompson's arm. "Let's finish ordering," she said gently, trying, as she almost always did, to step in between father and daughter before an argument could begin.

Kristin was grateful. Her father concentrated on explaining how he wanted his steak prepared, and before long the conversation turned to other topics. She began to relax a little. Sometimes it was hard to feel that she couldn't let up, not even for a second; that even while having dinner with her father and Dorrie she had to act the part of the pro. Almost-pro, she reminded herself.

But it was only a matter of minutes before the conversation turned back to tennis. "Did you see the article on Nick Wylie in the sports section today?" Neil Thompson asked his daughter. The waiter brought their salads, and Kristin took a quick bite before answering.

"I haven't seen the paper yet. I spent lunch hour trying to do some homework, and—"

"It was a fascinating article. Sounds like Wylie is exactly the kind of coach you need," Mr. Thompson interrupted her. "He's got a real eye for talent. The article talked about the Avery Cup tournament, too." He took a bite of his salad. "It's less than three weeks away now, Kristin. Are you feeling psyched up?"

Kristin poked at her salad with her fork. "I think so," she said feebly.

"But I haven't told you the best part," Mr.

Thompson went on. "Your name got mentioned. Someone did a story on the seventeen-and-under stars, and the writer went on and on about how wonderful you are. 'Strong, consistent, sure of herself,' the article said." He smiled affectionately at her. "I cut it out for your scrapbook."

"Thanks, Dad," Kristin murmured. She pushed her salad away, not feeling very hungry anymore. "Listen," she said suddenly, looking first at her father and then at Dorrie. "What would happen if—if something went wrong and I didn't make Nick Wylie's team?"

Mr. Thompson stared at her. "Honey, there's no way that's going to happen. You're a shoo-in. Who can possibly beat you?"

"That isn't the point," Kristin said desperately. "I just wondered what you two would do if something went wrong and I messed up and didn't make it."

"We wouldn't do anything, honey," Dorrie said. "What do you mean, do?"

Kristin blinked back tears. She needed badly to have her father's reassurance that he would love her every bit as much even if she didn't make the team. But Kristin knew that her tennis victories were important to him. For as long as she could remember, she had been his "star." Now she was going to help his biggest dream come true. If she made the all-star team, he would be the happiest man in the world—that's what he was always saying.

Mr. Thompson looked at her with concern. "Are you sure there isn't something that you're not telling us, Kristin? Did something upset you at school?"

Kristin shook her head and forced herself to keep eating. She didn't want to worry her father any more than she already had. All she wanted was to make him happy, to know that he and Dorrie were proud of her. She wasn't going to say a word about Emily Brown and the Big Sister program.

By the time Kristin and her father got home from the club, it was nearly eight-thirty. "I'm going upstairs to do my homework," Kristin told her father as she slipped out of her jacket.

Glancing at his watch, he nodded. "But don't stay up too late. Promise me you'll be in bed by ten-thirty."

Kristin nodded, trying to hide her annoyance. Didn't her father realize that she knew how much sleep she needed without having to be reminded?

"Remember, Kris, if you need anything at all in the next few weeks, just let me know," he continued, looking fondly at her. "Dorrie says she's completely at your disposal, too. If you want to spend more time practicing, we could even make arrangements with your teachers so you could spend some mornings at the club."

Kristin shook her head. "I don't think so, Dad. It's probably best for me to keep up my normal schedule." *And it would probably be best for me if you and Dorrie relaxed a little bit about this tournament,* she thought. *It's bad enough that I put pressure on myself without it coming from the two of you as well.*

"Sleep tight," he called as she hurried upstairs.

Kristin took a deep breath as she closed the bedroom door behind her and sank into the overstuffed chair next to her bed. She closed her eyes for a few minutes, trying to relax. At least her father cared passionately about tennis. Some of the other players didn't have their parents' support. Wouldn't that be a million times worse?

Deep down Kristin knew that her dad adored her and would do anything in the world for her. But sometimes she felt she would gladly exchange all her trophies for a normal life; to go out on dates, to parties, or to simply hang out with friends at school instead of spending every single minute of her life practicing.

She could remember, years back when she first started competing seriously, her father asking if this was what she really wanted. "Don't you want what other girls have?" he used to say. Kristin always said no. She wanted to be a great tennis player. Really great—world-class. While other girls her age were worrying about being asked to dances or getting their first formal dresses or falling in love or making friends, Kristin was worrying about strengthening her serve or getting her backhand in shape.

Kristin had done such a good job of convincing Dorrie and her father that tennis was all she wanted that neither of them would dream she might have reconsidered. Ages had passed since her father had asked if she missed doing things other girls her age did.

If the question came up again, Kristin wondered whether it would be possible to say that tennis was still all she wanted.

Her glance fell on a photograph on her nightstand. Kristin's eyes softened as she picked up the silver oval frame and gazed tenderly at her mother's image. It was her favorite picture of her mother; laughing, her head thrown back as she held the winning trophy of the U.S. Open in her arms. She looked so young and carefree in the photo. It was hard to believe that less than a year later she was dead.

Elise Randall had been a golden girl of tennis. Born and bred in California, she was a natural talent from the day she first picked up a racket. By the time she was sixteen she was slated to win Wimbledon one day. She won every match she played with effortless grace, which made reporters and fans adore her. She was so dedicated to tennis that when she finished high school, she decided not to go to college. By nineteen she had fallen in love with and gotten married to Neil Thompson, then a student at Stanford. When Neil graduated, he decided to borrow all the money he could to buy his first club. He and Elise wanted to start a series of tennis schools. They had all sorts of dreams, including having a family. When Kristin was born, they hoped she would be a pro, just like her mother. They bought her a racket as soon as she was big enough to hold it.

Kristin's memories of her mother were blurry. She remembered sitting on her father's lap, clapping when her mother won matches. She remembered the light, flowery smell of her mother's perfume when she came into Kristin's room in the middle of the night to kiss her after returning from whatever tour she had been on. And she remembered helping her mother pack before the trip to Wimbledon that was to claim her life. Her mother had been so excited. Wimbledon was the only competition left for her to win—the pinnacle she had worked for her whole life. "Someday you're going to be a champion, Kris," her mother had said fondly, rumpling her daughter's hair. "Then you'll know how I'm feeling today."

But the plane that was supposed to carry Elise to her greatest victory never landed in London. Something went wrong with the engine, and the plane crashed somewhere over the Atlantic. Kristin shuddered. Staring down at her mother's photograph, she remembered the nightmares she'd had that summer and fall. She would wake up screaming, and her heartbroken father would come running into her bedroom to gather her in his arms. But nothing worked. Kristin was inconsolable. She couldn't understand that her mother was gone for good.

For months after the accident, Kristin cried every time she saw a tennis racket. She wouldn't go to the club, and her grief was so evident that her teachers suggested she see a child psychologist to help her adjust to the terrible loss she had suffered.

Then one day, out of the blue, Kristin met her father at the club and told him she wanted to start lessons again. They never mentioned her mother. Kristin began to play with a passion that amazed her father and Dorrie. All she wanted was to play tennis—to win. It was as if her mother's words to her had turned into a final request: be like me. Be a champion. Win Wimbledon for me—the thing I could never do.

From that point on, tennis was Kristin's entire life. She played with a kind of earnestness that amazed her coaches. No one had ever seen such dedication or drive. They didn't know that Kristin was playing for her mother's memory. Only when she had a racket in her hand—only when she was winning—did it feel to Kristin that she hadn't really lost her mother. It was the only way she knew to keep her mother's spirit alive.

Four

"Elizabeth!" Kristin called, snapping the padlock on her bicycle shut. It was Tuesday morning, and Kristin wanted to catch Elizabeth before the first bell rang.

Elizabeth was walking with Jeffrey French across the lawn. She turned to Kristin with a quizzical smile.

"I want to talk to you about the Big Sister program," Kristin said breathlessly.

"Oh!" Elizabeth smiled at her. "Jeffrey, how 'bout if I find you later on?"

Jeffrey patted Elizabeth's hand affectionately before slipping off to leave the two girls alone to talk. Kristin felt a slight pang of envy. She wondered what it would be like to have a boyfriend, someone who knew every single thing that happened to you, someone as in love with you as Jeffrey was with Elizabeth.

She swallowed hard. "Jeffrey seems so nice," she said wistfully.

Elizabeth laughed. "He *is* nice," she said warmly.

Kristin took a deep breath. "Listen, I've given a lot of thought to being a big sister," she said carefully. "I have mixed feelings about it. On the one hand, I think it's a great idea, and I'd really like to sponsor Emily Brown."

"That's terrific!" Elizabeth broke in.

Kristin raised a hand in warning. "But my schedule is insane, Liz. Even under ordinary circumstances I wouldn't have time for this. I work out in the morning before school and every day after school till dinnertime. I do my homework in the evening, and my weekends are devoted to tennis." She frowned. "I don't want to let Emily down. If I sponsor her, she'll have to understand that I won't have as much time for her as I'd like to."

Elizabeth nodded thoughtfully. "I really appreciate your telling me in advance how busy you are." She thought for a minute. "Do you think you'd be able to see Emily once a week? That's what the foundation has asked us to be able to promise the girls. Remember," she added, "Emily might be thrilled just to come and practice with you."

"I hadn't thought of that," Kristin admitted. "I don't see why Emily couldn't come to practice with me whenever she wants! In fact, my schedule will slow down a little in about ten days. Do you know about the Avery Cup tournament?" she added.

"I've heard of it. Is it coming up?"

Kristin nodded. "I'm trying to qualify to play in it. If I make it—which I think I will—I'll be slowing down my practice schedule right before the tournament. That might be a really good time to get to know Emily better." She smiled. "So I guess I can do it after all!"

"Great. I know it will mean the world to this little girl," Elizabeth said.

Kristin nodded. What would her father and Dorrie think? Wasn't she picking the worst possible moment to make any sort of commitment outside of tennis?

But Kristin didn't care. Sponsoring Emily Brown in the Big Sister program was something she had to do. Whatever it took, she would find a way to make it fit into her schedule.

*   *   *

At the beginning of Kristin's last class, the teacher handed her a message that had been phoned in to the main office. It was from Dorrie. "I forgot to tell you I have a doctor's appointment this afternoon and won't be at the club until 4:30. See you then."

Kristin folded the note and put it in her pocket. Usually she met Dorrie at three-thirty. That meant she had a whole extra hour to herself, to do whatever she wanted.

Kristin started daydreaming about having every afternoon free. What a luxury it would be to wander off to the beach, get together with friends, or simply read a novel.

But when the class was over, Kristin suddenly didn't know what to do with herself. After all, an hour wasn't really long enough to go to the beach. She headed outside, watching groups of students joking around, getting into cars, and plopping down on the front lawn to enjoy the sun. Kristin tied her jacket around her waist and squinted into the sunlight. Well, she would just wander around for a while, she told herself.

Without really knowing where she was going, she strolled behind the school to the playing fields. She saw a small group gathered at the tennis courts and decided to watch whoever was playing.

At first she thought the blond at the front of the spectators was Elizabeth, but then she saw A. J. Morgan, who was in Kristin's English class, sitting next to her, and Kristin realized that the girl was Elizabeth's twin sister, Jessica. She knew the others only by name: Amy Sutton, Lila Fowler, and Cara Walker.

"Hi, Kristin," Cara and A.J. said when she wandered up to them.

"Hi," Kristin said shyly. She glanced at the court where two boys were warming up. "Who's playing?"

"Bruce Patman and Adam Tyner," Cara explained. "Bruce'll win for sure. He's really good."

Kristin looked curiously at Bruce. She had passed him a few times in the hallway, and he had talked to her briefly one day when she was hitting a few balls after school. He was strikingly good-looking, with the kind of dark, overpowering appearance that made a strong and immediate impression.

"And, boy, does he ever know it," Jessica complained. "I've played with Bruce a few times, and it's a real ordeal. He thinks he's such a star!"

Kristin's curiosity was piqued.

"Hey, Jess," Cara teased, "remember who you're talking to. Kristin's ball boys are better tennis players than Bruce Patman is!"

Jessica laughed. "That's right," she said affably to Kristin. "You're the one who's a star. Hey," she added, her eyes brightening, "you ought to play a quick game with Bruce and show him what real tennis is like!"

Kristin blushed. "No, that's OK," she said quickly.

But Jessica didn't let go of the idea. "Hey, Bruce," she called. "You've got a pro watching you now. Why don't you let her give you a few pointers?"

Bruce glared at Jessica, but his expression softened when he caught sight of Kristin. "Hi," he said, waving at her.

Kristin waved back and sat down on the grass to watch him play. If Bruce was embarrassed, he didn't show it. He wasn't a bad player, and he certainly outclassed his opponent by about a mile. He had a good strong serve and made some very nice, clean shots. Kristin found herself watching him the way she watched any tennis player—with an eye on his technique. She couldn't help noticing one or two areas of his game that needed some work.

When Bruce and Adam took a break, Bruce wandered over to Kristin, looking at her with interest. "So, champ," he said in a teasing voice, "how'd I do?"

Kristin looked at him seriously. "Not bad," she said. "But you'd do better if you kept your arm completely straight on your backhand. Also, you're taking two steps when you serve instead of one." She frowned. "And *always* keep your eye on the ball."

Bruce was silent for a minute. He rolled back and forth on his feet, looking at her. "Thanks," he said shortly, then turned back to Adam.

Kristin saw that he had paid attention to what she said. His next game was ten times better. He won by a satisfying margin.

"That was nice," she said calmly, when he walked over to her.

"Hey," Bruce said, clearing his throat, "why don't you hit a few balls with me? Let's see your stuff."

Kristin felt incredibly awkward. She had never played with anyone from school before. And even though Bruce was good, she could tell she would be able to beat him. "No, I really shouldn't," she murmured.

"Oh, come on," Bruce insisted. "Adam will lend you his racket. Just one game."

The crowd started to cheer, and finally Kristin agreed. "OK. But just one," she said uneasily, getting to her feet.

She felt strange facing Bruce across the net.

Adam's racket was heavier than the one she was used to, and she missed the first serve.

When her concentration came back, she hit two amazing volleys. Everyone cheered wildly, and Kristin felt the way she always felt when she was winning—wonderful.

Then something strange happened. She was watching Bruce bend for the ball, and it suddenly struck her how humiliated he was going to feel, losing to a girl in front of his friends. That was not the kind of thought Kristin usually had, but she had it then. At the same time she was thinking how handsome Bruce Patman was.

She let her next two serves go into the net. Then she flubbed a volley. Bruce ended up winning the game.

"Thanks," she said lightly. "You're a good player. You learn fast."

Bruce's eyes were fixed quizzically on hers. "I'm the one who should be saying thanks," he said as they shook hands. The pressure of his fingers made her face turn red.

She could tell that some of the spectators were surprised. Jessica looked especially disappointed. "I was sure you'd win," she said to Kristin.

Amy Sutton gave Kristin a chilly look. "I told you Bruce is incredibly good," she said imperiously.

Kristin looked uncertainly back at Bruce. He wasn't paying attention to what anyone was saying. His eyes were fixed on her, silently thanking her for letting him win.

"Well, thanks for the game," Kristin repeated awkwardly. "I have to get going now. I'm supposed to meet my coach at practice in about ten minutes."

Bruce grabbed his racket cover and started to follow her across the lawn. "Let me give you a ride," he offered. "I've never driven a real pro to practice before."

"I'm not a pro," Kristin said hastily. "Not yet." She smiled at him, her face feeling warm again. "And thanks for the offer, but I've got my bike here."

"You can come back for it later. Let me take you," Bruce pleaded. "I really want to."

Kristin was surprised. It was nice having Bruce pay so much attention to her. "OK," she said at last. She was stunned when the car Bruce led her to turned out to be a black Porsche.

"This is yours?" she asked incredulously. Kristin was so removed from school gossip that she knew very little about Bruce Patman. Well, now she knew he must come from an incredibly wealthy family.

Bruce seemed to enjoy her amazement. "Nice

little car, isn't it?" he said smoothly, opening the door for her.

Kristin got in without a word. She wondered what her father or Dorrie would say if they saw her being dropped off at the club in a Porsche, especially a Porsche driven by a boy who looked like Bruce.

"So how come I've hardly seen you around school?" Bruce was saying as he expertly backed the car out of the parking spot. "I know I would've made a point of spending time with someone as pretty as you."

Kristin felt her cheeks flame. No one had ever told her she was pretty before. "I, uh, practice a lot. And I do my homework during lunch hours," she blurted out.

Bruce laughed. "Bad habits," he remarked. "You'll have to take lessons on how to have a good time." He grinned lazily at her. "And I know just the person for those kinds of lessons."

Kristin swallowed hard. "I don't have much time," she repeated. "The Avery Cup tournament is coming up. If I qualify, I'm going to be under a lot of pressure for the next few weeks."

"Don't sweat it!" Bruce advised with a smile. "You'll qualify, and you'll win. You're a champ, Kristin." He stretched his right arm out so that it lay along the back of Kristin's seat. "I have a great idea," he said. "What are you doing this weekend?"

Kristin laughed. "Playing tennis," she said. Wasn't that what she did every single weekend?

"Don't tell me you play tennis Friday and Saturday nights!" Bruce exclaimed.

Kristin shrugged. "I do. Till about nine o'clock, anyway. And then I go to bed early so I can get up and practice again."

"Sounds like an incredible grind," Bruce said. He was still smiling, and Kristin couldn't tell whether or not he was kidding.

"If you want to be a pro, that's the kind of life you have to lead," she said matter-of-factly.

"Well, listen to me, pro," Bruce said, pulling the Porsche up in front of the club and turning to her with a grin. "How about taking one evening off and coming with me to see a movie on Friday night?"

Kristin stared at him wide-eyed. Was he asking her out on a date?

"Come on," he said again. "I won't take no for an answer."

Kristin could see Dorrie getting out of her station wagon in the parking lot. The last thing she wanted was for Dorrie to see her with Bruce.

"OK," she said hastily. "But I've got to get going now. That's my coach over there."

She didn't wait to hear Bruce's response. Kristin hurried out of the car, thinking that she would worry about Friday night when it rolled around. For now she had a bigger problem to face. It was 4:35, and for the first time in her whole life, Kristin was going to be late for practice.

Five

"I still don't see why you wouldn't let me pick you up at your house," Bruce complained. It was Friday evening, and Bruce had just picked Kristin up at a corner half a block from her house. They were headed to the Sweet Valley Cinema.

"Oh, I just thought this would be simpler," Kristin said. She didn't want to tell Bruce the truth—that her father would have objected if she had told him that she was going out on a date. He would have been concerned she was losing too much sleep before the tournament. So instead of a date, Kristin told him that she had to stop practicing early to do some research at the public library. "The library's open late on Friday nights," she had said. "And I can't get the books I need at school." Mr. Thompson hadn't looked thrilled. "I'm going out for a while myself," he'd said gruffly. "So I won't be home when you get back. But be sure you get to sleep early."

Kristin glanced sideways at Bruce. He seemed so sure of himself, so completely at ease. She didn't think he'd understand, and she didn't feel like explaining right now. "I have to be back early," was all she said with a rueful smile. "I have practice at nine o'clock tomorrow morning."

Bruce shook his head. "You have to learn how to relax," he scolded her lightly. "Don't you know there's more to life than tennis?" He gave her a warm smile, and she felt her cheeks flush.

That evening, for the first time she could remember, Kristin became convinced that Bruce might be right. She had so much fun joking around on the ticket line, sitting close to Bruce, and trading opinions when the movie ended. When Bruce reached over to hold her hand, it seemed like the most natural thing in the world. And Kristin was having so much fun she honestly didn't want to go home after the movie. But it was already ten o'clock, and she didn't know when her father was getting home. She wasn't going to make things worse by going to the Dairi Burger.

"No, Bruce, really," she protested. When he didn't seem to believe her, she added, "I'm under a lot of pressure right now. The Avery Cup means everything for my future. If I mess up at this tournament, my whole tennis career could be jeopardized. I have to be extra careful not to vary my routine too much for the next few weeks." She glanced down at the ground, embarrassed. "I had fun tonight, Bruce. I hope you'll be patient with me and give me another chance sometime."

"I guess I might," Bruce teased. "But I have to tell you, I'm not used to girls who have to be home by ten o'clock on a Friday night."

Kristin blushed deep red. "Sorry," she said, apologizing for seeming like a twelve-year-old. But deep down she knew she was right to insist on going home. If Bruce was worth getting to know, he would understand how much tennis meant to her. Still, Kristin couldn't help wishing she didn't have to live by a strict schedule.

When Bruce pulled up in front of Kristin's house, he turned to her and looked deeply into her eyes. "You're an amazing girl, Kristin. I've never met anyone like you before." He leaned over and kissed her lightly on the lips. "I'd like to see you again. I'm sure I'll be able to distract you, Kristin Thompson."

Kristin smiled nervously. Getting distracted was exactly what she was afraid of.

"Where are you going?" Jessica muttered sleepily at the breakfast table on Saturday morning.

"Over to the tennis club," Elizabeth explained as she slipped into her jacket and picked up her backpack.

"Mr. Collins wants me to write a special piece for the paper on Kristin and the Avery Cup tournament. I spoke to her father on the phone last night, and he said if I arrived a little before nine that I could ask her a few questions." She shook her head. "Kristin's got some schedule to follow! I don't see how anyone could be so disciplined."

Jessica groaned as she reached for a muffin. "I don't see how anyone can leave the house at this hour. I wouldn't have gotten up at all, except that I was hungry. I'm going back to bed as soon as I finish breakfast."

Elizabeth laughed. It was twenty-five minutes to nine when she left the house and drove off in the Fiat. She left the car in the club's parking lot and strolled out to the grass courts. Elizabeth noticed an attractive woman in tennis

47

whites who looked like she was waiting for someone. "Hello," Elizabeth said, introducing herself and explaining that she was with the school paper. "I was hoping to ask Kristin Thompson a little bit about the Avery Cup before she started practice," she said.

"I'm Dorrie Graham, Kristin's coach," the woman said with a warm smile. "Maybe I can give you some information while we wait for Kristin." She looked down at her watch with a frown. "It isn't like Kristin to be late. I know that her father gave her the message that you wanted to interview her."

"Well, maybe you could tell me a little bit about the Avery Cup selection process," Elizabeth said, taking out her notebook and sitting down on the bench.

She and Dorrie chatted for about five minutes, and Elizabeth took careful notes. She was going to ask about the history of the tournament when a handsome gray-haired man came striding toward them. "Good morning, Dorrie," he said. He smiled politely at Elizabeth, then looked around in confusion. "Where's Kristin?"

"I haven't seen her, Neil," Dorrie said. She glanced quickly at Elizabeth. "This is Elizabeth Wakefield, one of Kristin's classmates. She's here to interview Kristin before practice starts."

"Oh, yes. We spoke on the phone." Mr.

Thompson put out his hand to shake Elizabeth's. "Well, I don't know where she could be. I left her a note last night telling her that you'd be here, and I specifically asked her to get to practice early. I left home early to run some errands, and I thought she'd bike over."

Elizabeth smiled, slightly embarrassed by the critical tone in his voice. "I'm not in any hurry," she said quickly. "I don't mind waiting."

But Mr. Thompson was clearly upset. "It isn't like Kristin to be late," he said, annoyed. He looked quizzically at Dorrie. "Did she tell you she had somewhere to go this morning?"

"Neil," Dorrie said softly, "it's just a little past nine now. She'll be here."

Elizabeth noticed with relief that Kristin was hurrying toward them. She couldn't believe what a big deal Mr. Thompson was making about his daughter being a few minutes late, and it made her curious about Kristin. How could she stand having her father and Dorrie hover over her that way? Or was that just part of what it meant to be a dedicated athlete?

"I'm really sorry," Kristin said, pushing her hair back from her face. "I overslept!" She looked sheepishly from her father to Dorrie. "I didn't hear the alarm."

"Well, it's not the end of the world," Dorrie

said, patting her on the arm. "You're here now, aren't you?"

But Mr. Thompson was frowning at her. "Maybe you're not getting enough sleep," he said with concern. "Did you get to bed early enough last night?"

Kristin looked away as she said, "Yes, I was in bed by eleven." Which was the truth. What she couldn't tell her father was that she was so excited about having gone out on a date that she had laid in bed, thinking about it, unable to sleep. She had still been awake at one o'clock.

Turning to Elizabeth, Kristin said, "I'm afraid I've messed things up for you, too," she murmured. "I really need to start practice soon, so we won't have that much time for your interview."

"Oh, go ahead," Dorrie said, giving both girls a smile. "I don't see why we can't relax our schedule this once. I tell you what, Kristin. I'll go and have a cup of coffee with your dad while you two talk. We can get started in half an hour. How does that sound?"

Kristin gave her a grateful smile. "Phew," she whispered when Dorrie and her father moved out of earshot. She turned to Elizabeth. "That was a close one. My dad is an unbelievable stickler when it comes to my practice schedule. He's always said, 'Stars aren't born, they're trained.' " She plopped down next to Elizabeth on the bench. "I'm not supposed to go out, and I had a date last night. I got home early, but it wouldn't have been early to him if he had known. But he was out."

Elizabeth raised her eyebrows. She felt she was learning a lot more about Kristin Thompson than she had expected to. "Is your dad pretty strict about stuff like that?" she asked. She was wondering where Kristin's mother was but felt it wasn't right to ask.

"Well—is this off the record? I wouldn't want any of this to go into the school paper," Kristin said slowly.

Elizabeth nodded. "Fine. Why don't we just talk for a little while. I'll ask you questions, and when I've written up the interview I'll show it to you. You can veto anything that seems too personal."

Kristin relaxed a little. "He *is* strict," she admitted. "Not strict because he doesn't want me to go out, but strict because he's a fanatic about tennis. He really wants me to turn pro." She sighed. "In fact, my dad's been more psyched about my tennis career than I've been—well, almost."

Elizabeth was surprised. "That seems pretty unusual. Is that because he owns tennis clubs?"

Kristin hesitated a moment, then said, "Well,

partly. My mother played tennis, too," she blurted out. "She was killed in an accident when I was seven." She sighed and stared down at her hands. "Tennis was the one thing Dad and I had that made it seem like she was still around. Does that make sense?"

Elizabeth nodded. "Yes, it makes sense," she said gently. "Kristin, that must have been so hard for you!"

Kristin's face was perfectly composed as she faced Elizabeth. "It *was* hard," she said matter-of-factly. "To tell you the truth, that was why I was willing to help you in the Big Sister program. I thought Emily's situation was similar to what mine had been. I wanted to try to help her out."

Elizabeth's eyes filled with compassion. "By the way, I have good news. Emily's counselor contacted us yesterday, and you've been made her official sponsor." She handed Kristin an envelope from her backpack. "Here's all the material you'll need on her—her address, her phone number, stuff about her school and her other interests. You can call her whenever you want to."

Kristin thanked her. "I'll call her this weekend," she promised.

Elizabeth glanced down at the list of questions she had prepared. After asking a few, she got the impression that Kristin was saying things by rote, rather than from her heart. For each of the questions she had prepared, Kristin had the expected answer. She described her training in a detached tone that made it sound like someone else's schedule. When Elizabeth asked, "Do you ever miss doing normal things, leading the kind of life most kids your age lead?" Kristin just shook her head.

"No," she said automatically, squinting out at the tennis courts. "I want to be a pro. Tennis is my whole life. It's all that counts."

Elizabeth detected a flat, slightly unnatural tone in Kristin's voice. She didn't believe it was all as straightforward as Kristin made it seem. Surely an enormous amount of hard work and many sacrifices had enabled Kristin to excel in tennis. Elizabeth couldn't believe that there weren't times when Kristin felt regrets or ambivalence about having tennis dominate her life.

But Kristin certainly didn't reveal any of that to Elizabeth. "I hate to sound boring, but that's really all there is to it," she said when the interview was concluded. "About a hundred and ten percent tennis. Not too thrilling, right?"

Elizabeth closed her notebook with a smile. "I wouldn't apologize for being dedicated, Kristin. I think you're a great example of what it takes to be a winner." She reached out to shake

Kristin's hand. "And I think Emily Brown is going to learn a lot from you."

As Elizabeth walked off the court, she couldn't help but wonder if Kristin was happy to be playing tennis. She could tell how devoted she was and how much it meant to her to win, but she couldn't tell whether tennis gave her any joy. Elizabeth had a suspicion that tennis filled a void in Kristin's life.

Six

Mr. Thompson was out on the patio, drinking iced tea and reading the newspaper, when Kristin got home from practice. Kristin joined him and plopped down on a chaise longue. "It's nice out here," she said, stretching out with a comfortable sigh. She felt good. Practice had gone better that day, and she felt as though she had really earned the praise Dorrie had given her.

"Now, go home and rest up," Dorrie had instructed with a teasing smile, pretending to shoo her away. The first round of qualifying matches for the Avery Cup was being held on Tuesday, just three days away. That meant slowing down her practice schedule to store up energy.

Mr. Thompson lowered his paper and regarded his daughter with a mixture of curiosity, concern, and annoyance. "Kristin, a boy called to speak to you. Twice, in fact. Bruce Patman."

Kristin felt her cheeks turn red. "Oh," she said, half-pleased and half-embarrassed. "What did he want?"

"He left a bunch of phone numbers and asked you to call him back. I couldn't keep track of which was which. I think one was his club, and unless I heard wrong, another was his car phone." Mr. Thompson was staring at her. "Who is Bruce Patman, Kris?"

"Just a guy at school," Kristin said noncommittally. "He's a friend, Dad."

"Well, there's nothing wrong with that," Mr. Thompson said, turning back to his paper. "I just wondered why you'd never mentioned him, that's all."

Kristin knew she had hurt his feelings by shutting him out. Right now, however, she didn't want to share Bruce Patman with anyone. "I'm going up to take a shower," she said, getting up as casually as she could.

Once in her room, she called Bruce, wrinkling her nose a little bit at the thought of a car phone. The Patmans seemed to have an unlimited amount of money, and Kristin was beginning to suspect that Bruce had an unlimited ego as well. She'd had a lot of fun the night before, but thinking about it later, she realized the conversation had centered mostly on Bruce.

Still, it was flattering to think he was interested in her. His voice sounded warm and affectionate over the phone. "Kristin!" he exclaimed. "I've been waiting to hear from you. I want you to come over tonight to see the new set of speakers my dad just bought me. They're amazing. Top of the line—totally fantastic sound. And I just picked up some new compact discs, so you'll really hear some great music."

Kristin fiddled with the phone cord. "Uh—thanks, Bruce, but I can't."

"Don't tell me." Bruce groaned. "You're practicing tennis on a *Saturday night.*"

Kristin had to laugh at how outraged he sounded. "Actually, I'm not. But I'm having dinner with my coach and my dad. Besides, I have to be up at the crack of dawn tomorrow."

"So, you seriously can't come over tonight because you're having dinner with your father?" Bruce asked incredulously.

"That's right." Kristin laughed at how shocked he sounded. "Try giving me a little more notice next time, OK?"

Bruce was about to say something more, but Kristin cut him off. "I have to go," she said, picking up Emily Brown's telephone number. "There's somebody else I have to call."

Emily Brown was sitting on her front porch waiting for Kristin when she arrived at eight-thirty the next morning. Emily was small for a nine-year-old. She had smooth brown hair, cut fairly short, dark brown eyes, and a shy, slightly closed-off expression. There was something sad about her that made Kristin's heart ache. Seeing Emily was like looking back in time to the small scared child she had been.

"Hi, Emily," Kristin said, walking toward the front steps with a warm smile. "I'm Kristin."

Emily smiled shyly, afraid to raise her eyes. "Hi," she whispered. Just then, Mr. Brown came out and Kristin introduced herself. "I'm taking Emily to my dad's tennis club," she said. "I'll bring her back this afternoon."

Emily gave her father a quick kiss goodbye, then ran down the porch steps to Kristin. "Are we *really* going to a tennis club?" she asked, wide-eyed.

"We sure are," Kristin said, taking Emily by the hand. She was astonished by how small it was.

Emily was staring at her. "Do you really play in tournaments?" she demanded.

Kristin laughed. "Yep. I'll show you my trophies later on if you want."

Emily's eyes lit up. "Yeah!" she exclaimed.

Kristin chattered as they drove to the club. She told Emily how the club was run, how classes worked, and what her own training was like. Emily was quiet, but Kristin could tell that she was listening avidly.

"Now, promise you'll tell me if you get bored. The minute you want to go home, we'll leave," Kristin said when they got to the club.

"I won't get bored," Emily declared, her eyes shining.

Sunday morning was magical for Kristin. Seeing the club through Emily's eyes reminded her of the way she had felt when she had first started playing—the thrill of meeting a real coach, the excitement of going into the pro shop and handling the balls and rackets, the newness of it all. Emily kept saying how "cool" everything was. And when they walked down the main hallway and Emily saw the signed photograph of Kristin taken at the Junior Open the year before, her eyes got as big as saucers. "You're really famous!" she exclaimed to Kristin. The next minute she slid her tiny hand back inside Kristin's.

"Looks like someone around here has a new friend," Dorrie said, giving Kristin a wink and bending down to ruffle Emily's hair.

"Listen," Kristin said, bending down so she could look at Emily eye to eye. "I'm going to have to start practice in a little while. But before I do, how would you like to hit a few balls with me? That way I can see what stage you're at and maybe give you a couple of pointers."

Emily was beside herself. "I get to hit balls with Kristin!" she cried to Dorrie. She was practically hugging herself from the excitement.

Kristin grinned down at her. It was amazing how much the little girl had come alive during their first morning together. Becoming Emily's big sister was one of the best decisions Kristin had ever made.

"Bruce called again," Mr. Thompson commented when Kristin opened the front door early that evening. Kristin had ended up spending the day with Emily. After calling Mr. Brown to tell him they would be late, Kristin had taken Emily to dinner at the club.

"Oh, thanks," Kristin said, hoping her voice sounded casual.

"Listen, doesn't a father get to hear the details anymore?" Mr. Thompson joked. "Bruce must be pretty interested if he's called you three times in one weekend."

Kristin blushed. "I guess so. But it's hard to tell, Dad." She shrugged out of her jacket. "Bruce is a senior. He could go out with anyone he wants to. I don't understand why he's calling me."

Mr. Thompson shook his head. "Kristin, Kristin," he said with a sigh. "Didn't I tell you that when you hit sixteen you'd have more requests for dates than you'd know what to do with?"

Kristin sneaked a glance at herself in the hallway mirror. She saw the same old Kristin—baggy sweats, her face showing a few freckles from the sun—not exactly a glamour girl.

"Anyway," Mr. Thompson went on, "you probably don't need my advice, but I hope your new friendship won't interfere with the Avery Cup."

Kristin's jaw squared slightly. She had been just about ready to say that she was too busy right now to see Bruce, but the fact that her father had said it first irritated her. Didn't he think she knew her training schedule well enough to make her own decisions?

"I can't really see how it would," she said lightly, her voice cool. Mr. Thompson didn't answer. She could tell she had hurt him, but Kristin couldn't help it. The Avery Cup was *her* tournament, not his! She didn't see why her father couldn't give her a little more space to make her own decisions.

"I'm going to call Bruce back," she said, trying to keep her expression neutral. Only her shaking hands revealed how much the exchange had upset her. Ever since she could remember, she and her father had been arguing about her schedule. Deep down they both wanted the same thing, but Kristin wanted the freedom to choose tennis, not to have it chosen for her!

Ten minutes later she had reached Bruce.

"I happen to be having an amazing ice-cream fit," Bruce told her. "If I don't get a massive amount of mocha-double-Oreo-fudge into my system within twenty minutes, I might self-destruct."

Kristin giggled. Bruce might be arrogant and spoiled, but she liked his sense of humor. "I'm not supposed to eat any ice cream," she said wistfully. "My favorite is double-cheesecake with nuts."

"Why aren't you supposed to eat ice cream? A girl like you needs energy!" Bruce cried. "Look, I'll be over in five minutes. That means if we drive really fast, we'll make it to Casey's before I explode." He hung up before she had time to turn him down.

Kristin was still giggling a few minutes later. She went over to the dresser and brushed her auburn hair. Then she went downstairs to tell her father where she was going.

"Ice cream? Is that on your diet?" Mr. Thompson asked mildly.

"I can probably manage one scoop," Kristin said lightly. "I'll be home really early, Dad. We're just going straight there and back. I probably won't be gone more than an hour."

Mr. Thompson frowned. "Just don't be late," he said, not meeting her eyes. "You know how much you need to get a good night's sleep right now. The first match is only two days away."

"I know, Dad," Kristin said patiently. It took all her self-control not to add, "After all, I'm the one in the tournament, remember?"

"Listen, Casey's is totally beat," Bruce said as soon as Kristin had snapped on her seat belt. "I've got a much better idea. There's an incredible little café in the canyon that's also a jazz club. A tenor sax player from L.A. is playing there tonight. I've been wanting to hear him. Let's go there instead."

Kristin frowned. "I really shouldn't, Bruce. It sounds like fun, but I really can't be out very late. And—"

But Bruce was already turning the key in the ignition. "Trust me," he said cheerfully, pulling the car out of the driveway. "We'll be back before you know it."

Kristin sat back, feeling helpless. There wasn't much she could do to stop Bruce. She would just have to hope it didn't take more than an hour.

"Kristin?" Mr. Thompson was waiting for her in the living room. The mantel clock was just chiming the half hour: ten-thirty.

"Dad, look, I'm so sorry—"

"I've been worried sick," Mr. Thompson cut her off. "You promised me you'd be back in an hour, and then you show up three hours late."

Kristin took a deep breath. "We ended up going somewhere different than—"

"I'm disappointed in you, Kristin," Mr. Thompson interrupted again. "I didn't think I needed to say this, but maybe I do. I've watched you work for years and years for the opportunity to join the pro circuit. Now I'm seeing you throw it all away. You aren't even bothering to take care of yourself before the biggest tournament of your life. Doesn't this tournament matter to you anymore?"

Kristin felt as if she had been slapped. She couldn't answer.

"That's all I have to say to you. Now, I'm

going to bed," Mr. Thompson said heavily. "And I suggest you do the same."

Kristin didn't say a word. She just stared at his back as he walked out of the room. If only she could explain that the tournament did matter to her—more than anything in the whole world—but that she also wanted to see what it felt like to be a normal teenager.

Seven

Kristin took a deep breath. For as long as she could remember, she had had her own special way of getting psyched up before a match. She tried to block out every single thought in her head and just focus on how badly she wanted to win.

Mr. Thompson and Emily were among the crowd that had gathered to watch the first round of qualifying matches. Emily held up a Go Kristin sign and waved it around in the air.

Kristin took another breath. She had ten minutes before her match.

"Betsy shouldn't give you any trouble," Dorrie

said confidently, her arm draped around Kristin's shoulder as they walked back and forth on the side of the farthest court. Betsy Weber was seeded well below Kristin, and everyone was confident Kristin would win.

Kristin narrowed her eyes, trying not to watch Betsy warming up and talking to her coach. She knew she shouldn't exert too much mental energy trying to size up her competition until she had her racket in her hand and was squaring off at the net.

"I'm glad Emily's here," she said suddenly.

Dorrie smiled at her. "She's a sweet little girl. I think you're doing her a world of good, spending some time with her."

A strange thought came to Kristin then. "Maybe she's doing *me* a world of good," she said. Dorrie looked surprised, but there wasn't time to say more. The referees were calling them over. It was time for the match to begin.

Usually Kristin relaxed after the first serve, but today it seemed to take her longer to get into her rhythm. She missed several easy shots and ended up losing the first game.

"Just relax," Dorrie instructed, hurrying over with a towel before the second game. "Is the sun getting in your eyes? You looked uncomfortable to me."

Kristin shook her head, wiping her hands

furiously on her white shorts. "I'm OK. Just a little tense," she said uncertainly. She could see her father frowning from the sidelines.

"Well, take it easy," Dorrie said lightly. "Remember, you've played Betsy before—and beaten her easily. Just take your time and have fun out there."

Kristin nodded, but her mouth felt dry. She tried to remember what it felt like to have fun on the court. Reporters had always said she made winning look like child's play, but today it was incredibly hard work. Kristin won the first set, 7–5, but she was completely worn out, her face red and her breathing ragged.

Dorrie came over with a towel again. "Well done," she said, giving her a hug.

Kristin mopped her face off, trying to catch her breath. "I'm playing so badly," she moaned. "I don't know what's wrong with me."

"Look, you're ahead," Dorrie said lightly. "Try not to be so hard on yourself."

But Kristin knew her game was off. Beating Betsy wasn't supposed to be difficult. What was going to happen to her on Thursday, *if* she got to the second qualifying rounds?

The second set was a little better, but Kristin was still double-faulting on her service games. She felt rusty and awkward, as if she hadn't played tennis in months. Competition usually brought her a surge of adrenaline, but today Kristin was in a real slump. Every single shot was hard won. It felt like a miracle to her when she finally won the second set. The match was hers.

"You played well," Kristin gasped to Betsy, climbing over the net to shake her hand.

Betsy wiped her forehead. "Not well enough," she said ruefully. "Good game, Kristin." She looked disappointed, but at the same time her gaze was admiring. "I hope you make it all the way. You deserve to be on Wylie's team."

Kristin bit her lip. Betsy's compliment showed real sportsmanship, but Kristin knew she hadn't played very well. If she couldn't get her game back up to scratch, she didn't deserve to play on anyone's team, let alone Nick Wylie's pro circuit.

Reporters, coaches, and other people crowded close to shake Kristin's hand, congratulating her and asking questions about the second round of matches. On Thursday, Kristin would be playing Wendy Gibson, the fifth seed.

"Are you worried about Thursday's match?" a reporter asked.

Kristin opened her mouth to answer. The automatic response—"No, I'm looking forward to it. It should be a good match"—suddenly seemed to vanish. For a crazy minute she felt like saying, "Yes, I am worried. To tell you the truth, I didn't play very well just now, and I'm afraid if I don't get my act together between now and then, I'll lose—and break my father's heart."

But she didn't say anything. She just stared at the reporter.

Luckily Dorrie broke in to run interference. "We're expecting a good fight on Thursday," she said briskly, putting her arm around Kristin and steering her through the crowd.

"You played great," Dorrie said, squeezing her warmly.

Kristin shook her head. "No, I didn't," she protested. "Dorrie, I was terrible out there! I felt like my legs were made out of lead."

Before Dorrie could respond, Emily came running up, Kristin bent down, and the little girl threw her arms around Kristin. "You won! You won!" she cried. "Krissy, I'm so proud of you!"

Kristin clutched the girl tightly. She could feel her tiny heart beating fast against her own. She didn't think she could bear to look her in the face. Emily thought she was some kind of heroine, and the truth was, she had barely won a match that should have been hers without the slightest effort.

She couldn't bear the thought of letting any of them down on Thursday. Not Dorrie, not her father, and not poor Emily. Here they all were, thinking she was so wonderful. But what if she lost on Thursday? What if they all found out that she wasn't a winner after all?

Mr. Thompson didn't say anything to Kristin about the match, but she knew he was worried. They were both silent most of the way home, and after they dropped Emily off, Kristin felt an almost overwhelming desire to tell him how upset she was.

"Dad—" she started to say.

But he cut her off. "I think you're just under a lot of strain," he said absentmindedly. He turned to her with a look of such confusion and concern that she wanted to cry. "How about taking a vacation together, just you and me, after the tournament is over? I know once you've made the team you'll be able to relax a little. You'll really deserve a break."

Kristin felt her eyes fill with tears. *What if I don't win?* she was thinking. *Won't I need—and deserve—a break anyway?* But she didn't have the courage to ask him. She just slumped back in the car seat and stared miserably through the front window.

"I want you to get a lot of rest the next couple of nights," Mr. Thompson continued. "No more evening dates. Your match with Wendy is going to be pretty tough on Thursday. And after that—"

"Daddy," Kristin moaned. She felt so tense, and she was afraid she was going to break down in sobs. "I know how much sleep I need. Remember, I'm the one who's playing in this tournament!"

Kristin couldn't believe the words she had blurted out. Her father looked shocked and hurt. Kristin felt terrible, but she couldn't help feeling angry with Dorrie for telling her she had played well when she knew she hadn't. And now she was angry with her father's understated criticism.

Kristin could feel the blood pounding in her ears. The truth was that she just didn't know what *she* wanted anymore.

"Kristin, it's for you," Mr. Thompson called from downstairs that evening.

Kristin frowned. She pushed aside the second draft of her essay on "The American Dream" and picked up the phone.

"Kris? It's Bruce."

Kristin swallowed. She didn't know if she

was glad to hear from him or not. For one thing, she hated being called Kris by anyone other than her father or Dorrie. And Bruce sounded so darned sure of himself. "Hi," she said flatly, sitting down on the edge of her bed and twisting the cord with her fingers.

Bruce launched into a long monologue. "I wanted to find you today in school to wish you luck on your match, but I had to take my car to the shop at lunchtime—nothing serious, luckily—and then I ran into a couple of guys and got totally sidetracked after school. I was thinking about you the whole time, though. I knew you'd win."

Kristin kept fiddling with the phone cord. "Yeah," she said dryly. She hadn't really expected Bruce to come to the match, but she didn't think he had to go on and on making excuses, either.

"Anyway," Bruce rushed on, "I'm calling because I've got something incredibly, unbelievably important to talk to you about. Are you busy this Saturday night?"

Kristin took a deep breath. "Yes—" she started to say.

"Well, you'll just have to cancel whatever you're doing," he interrupted cheerfully, "because I happen to be asking you to go to my parents' enormous annual blowout bash they're springing at the country club this Saturday. I would've asked you sooner, but I had to clear it with them," he added. "I mean, Kristin, this is *the* party of the year. It's just amazing. And I've got to have you there by my side. I just have to."

Kristin was surprised. She had heard one or two kids at school talking about the Patmans' party, and she had wondered whether or not Bruce would mention it to her. But the thought of actually being his date . . . well, it was pretty flattering. For a brief moment Kristin thought how cool it would be to show up at the party of the year as the host's date. She had never done anything like it. But she also knew it would be impossible.

"I can't," she said stoically. "Sunday morning is the third round of qualifying matches for the Avery Cup. If I make it past Thursday, I'll have to be in bed really early Saturday night."

Bruce didn't seem perturbed. "Come on," he said. "You're going to win this thing with one hand tied behind your back! What you'll need to do on Saturday night is relax, not sit home worrying about the next morning. Please, Kristin," he cajoled. "I really want you to be there." When she didn't respond, he added, dropping his voice a little, "I told my parents about you. They're really looking forward to meeting you."

"Let me think about it," Kristin said. She couldn't believe she was reconsidering Bruce's invitation. There was no question what she ought to do! Yet Kristin wanted to be at the party—as Bruce's date. She was very tempted to tell him yes.

Eight

"I've been thinking," Jessica said, finishing the last bite of a chocolate-chip cookie at lunch. "Wouldn't it be a great idea if we got some kind of award for who was doing the best job with her little sister?"

Cara laughed. "I don't think it's supposed to be competitive, Jess. I think the whole point is just to have a good time and try to help the little girls out."

Jessica flipped back her hair. "I don't mean to brag," she said cheerfully, "but I've already done two things with Allison Post."

Lila cracked up. "You probably took her to

the beach once and went to the mall afterward. Right?"

Jessica gave her friend a cool look. "In fact, we happen to be going to the mall this afternoon, after school. I need to find something to wear to the Patmans' party, and I thought it might be fun for Allison to come along."

"Yeah"—Amy Sutton giggled—"Allison can run back and forth and bring you different sizes and stuff."

Jessica ignored her. "And then afterward we're baking cookies with Liz and *her* little sister, Kim Edgars. By the way, what are you all doing about dresses? Are you wearing formals?"

Amy suddenly looked perturbed. "I'm kind of irritated with Bruce. He's been telling me about this party for ages, and all of a sudden he's clammed up. I don't even know if he still thinks I'm going to be his date."

Jessica and Lila exchanged glances. Bruce had dated Amy a few times in the past, but she acted as if they'd had a real relationship. Bruce had only ever seriously dated one girl, Regina Morrow, and her tragic death from trying cocaine had affected the whole school. Now Bruce was back to playing the field, but the merest suggestion that he might be interested in someone else was enough to drive Amy crazy.

"Anyway, I saw this really filmy peach-colored

dress at Lisette's that I'm going to buy," Amy concluded. She stood and picked up her tray, then said smugly, "Even if he's been kind of distant lately, one look at me in that dress and Bruce Patman will be out of his mind with love!"

Lila waited until Amy was out of earshot before turning to Jessica. "Is it true Bruce asked Kristin Thompson to his party?" she demanded.

Jessica shrugged. "That's what A.J. told me. He said Bruce was bragging about it to a bunch of guys in gym class today, saying how even though Kristin is competing in a big tournament, she's still willing to drop everything and come to his party."

Lila let out a low whistle. "Wow," she said. "I can't wait to see sparks fly when Amy shows up on Saturday and realizes she isn't Bruce's date!"

Wendy Gibson was playing incredibly well. Kristin wiped her hand on her tennis skirt and tried not to let her feelings show as she ran back to the service line. It was the middle of the first set, and Wendy was winning, four games to three. The score now was 40–30, Wendy's lead. After a particularly intense volley, Kristin tried a lob shot, but it was long.

"Game!" Wendy cried, throwing her racket in the air.

Kristin had to blink back tears. It was five games to three now, and she felt she was losing her psychological advantage. Kristin knew she would have a tough time catching up unless she got a grip on her nerves and began to play more aggressive and accurate tennis.

Despite hard work in the next game, though, Kristin lost the set. She could barely look Dorrie in the eye at the break.

"Kristin, what is it? What's going on?" Dorrie asked, her mild voice betraying legitimate worry.

Kristin took a deep breath. "I don't know. I just don't seem to be able to keep up my concentration. And Wendy's playing incredibly well," she added. It was unlike Kristin to make excuses, but suddenly she felt exhausted—physically and emotionally. She felt like walking off the court. "Look," she said, struggling for control, "I'm going to give this everything I've got. That's all you can ask for, right?"

Dorrie didn't answer for a minute. "Not when you're a pro, kiddo," she said finally. "When you're a pro, you've got to give everything you've got as a baseline. Then the work starts."

Kristin turned away, her eyes swimming with tears. She knew Dorrie was right. As a coach, Dorrie should have been psyching Kristin up, not sympathizing with her. But all of a sudden

Kristin felt an incredible need for someone to be there who loved her just for who she was, not for her tennis. Someone to give her a simple hug.

"OK," she said, trying to force a smile. "Here goes nothing."

Using every bit of strength Kristin had, she managed to win the second set. It was close, and by the end both girls were panting and red-faced. A crowd had gathered to watch their last set. Whichever girl won would be in the final qualifying match on Sunday morning.

Kristin won the first two games. Then Wendy won one. Kristin another. Soon it was five games to three, and Kristin knew all she had to do was win one more game to win the match. Her shoulder felt like it was on fire when she served, and it was hard for her to keep her eyes focused on the ball. But she did it. She won the last game.

"Well done," Wendy said, not even bothering to hide her disappointment when they shook hands.

Kristin wiped her brow with a trembling hand. "You played well," she gasped.

Wendy had played well, but Kristin knew that her own game had been just so-so. At this rate she wasn't going to stand a chance against Sharon Owens on Sunday morning.

Dorrie put her arm around her as they walked to the clubhouse together. "What happened out there today?" she asked in a calm, controlled voice. "I thought I saw you start to panic in the middle of the second set. Let's go through it so it doesn't have to happen again."

Kristin shook her head. "Can we wait to talk? I'm just totally wiped out, Dorrie."

Dorrie nodded, but there was a look of disappointment in her eyes. Kristin had dreaded a moment like this for as long as she could remember. Dorrie's look said, clear as day, "You've let me down."

Suddenly something snapped in Kristin, and she broke away from Dorrie's light embrace. "All you and Daddy care about is tennis," she cried. "Just for once, can't you love me and support me regardless of whether or not I win?"

Dorrie looked at her in complete astonishment. Before she could say a word, Kristin broke into a run toward the clubhouse. All she wanted right then was to be alone.

"Wow!" Kim Edgars exclaimed when she saw the Wakefields' Spanish-tiled kitchen. "This is fantastic! Is this where we're baking cookies?"

Elizabeth nodded. "It sure is. Only remember," she added, her eyes sparkling, "we're having a bake-a-thon against Jessica and Allison. Whoever bakes the most cookies the fastest—and the best—is the winner."

Jessica and Allison were already taking out ingredients and setting them up on the counter. "What does the winner get?" Jessica demanded.

Elizabeth laughed. "The winners don't have to clean up. And the losers"—she winked at Kim—"have to clean everything. Spick and span."

Jessica was frowning at the recipe. "This is way too complicated, Allison. Should we try a shortcut? I know we can beat them if—" She bent closer to the little girl and whispered something in her ear, and Allison giggled.

Elizabeth shook her head. "Not a very good idea," she said reproachfully. "Kim, what do you think? Should we follow the recipe or take a shortcut?"

The twins' mother, Alice Wakefield, who had just come into the kitchen, wanted to know what was going on, and soon the twins had convinced her to be the judge. "You have to decide whose cookies are better," Jessica declared. "We can figure out who makes more and who's faster, but you have to be the quality control."

Mrs. Wakefield laughed ruefully. "Why am I afraid that whoever gets the clean-up chore is in for a big job?"

For the next hour the kitchen was filled with frenetic activity as the twins and their two young helpers whipped up batches of batter and raced back and forth to the oven with trays of chocolate-chip cookies. Jessica and Allison were far ahead when it came to speed, but Kim and Elizabeth agreed that their opponents' cookies looked strangely pale. "They're leaving out some of the ingredients," Kim cried.

Elizabeth burst out laughing. "Jess, what are you two doing?" she cried. "Aren't you putting in brown sugar or chocolate chips or any of that stuff?"

"We're trying to hurry," Jessica said, miffed. "Just wait and see. I bet Mom thinks ours are every bit as good as yours are."

Elizabeth gave Kim a *v*-for-*victory* sign behind the counter. "My sister," she whispered, "is a crazy woman."

Kim giggled, covering her mouth with her hand. Elizabeth felt warm inside, knowing how much fun the two girls were having. Jessica, too, seemed to be enjoying herself. Elizabeth could hardly believe it when Mrs. Wakefield called, "Time!"

Allison and Jessica had managed to bake fifty cookies in an hour, whereas Elizabeth and Kim only had three dozen.

"We won! We won!" Jessica cried, dancing around the kitchen with her arms around Allison.

"Now, wait a minute," Mrs. Wakefield objected. "Each of you choose a cookie and let me taste," she said to Allison and Kim.

Elizabeth cracked up when she saw the pale cookie Allison selected. Everyone laughed when Mrs. Wakefield took a bite of it and spat it out. "Ugh," she cried. "What's in this thing?"

"See!" Elizabeth cried happily, giving Kim a hug. "You've heard of the tortoise and the hare, right? Well, it obviously applies to cookie-baking, too. Kim, we may be slower, but our cookies taste better."

Jessica and Allison looked sorrowfully at the mess they had made, and neither Elizabeth nor Kim could contain their giggles any longer. "Should we help them, or make them do it all themselves?" Elizabeth asked her brand-new little sister.

Kim smiled impishly. "I guess we could help—a little," she said. She went over to Allison, and the two girls picked up some dirty bowls to carry to the sink. From the way they grinned at each other, another new friendship seemed to have formed.

Elizabeth chuckled. "I'm only willing to help clean up on one condition. Jess, I want to see you eat one of your own cookies!"

Jessica tried to look nonchalant, but she wasn't fooling any of them. "I would," she said casually, "but I just happen not to be very hungry."

Mrs. Wakefield burst out laughing, and Kim and Allison looked at each other, and both started giggling.

That night Mr. Thompson had invited Dorrie over to the house for dinner. At first Kristin thought she couldn't bear to face her coach after her disappointing match, but as they sat down to eat, she realized it was a relief having Dorrie there. As usual, it was impossible for Kristin to relate to her father without Dorrie's help.

"The thing is not to panic," Neil Thompson was saying. "I was talking to another coach about it today, and it's apparently one of the most natural phenomena in tennis. You take someone like Kristin—someone who's been under so much pressure all her life, working so hard for this goal—and it often happens that when she gets very close to making it, she'll clutch."

Kristin poked at her food, hating this. How could they talk about her as though she wasn't even there?

Dorrie seemed to guess how she was feeling. "It's been a rough year for you, hasn't it?" she said gently, turning to Kristin.

Kristin pushed her vegetables from one side

of the plate to the other. "Look," she said, "it's just that I sometimes think I wouldn't mind having a more normal life. I'd like to have more time to be with friends, to be with Emily. Or to go out on dates," she blurted.

Mr. Thompson frowned. "I hope none of this has to do with that new friend of yours, Bruce," he said heavily. "I don't blame you for feeling some resistance every now and then, but to throw away a lifetime of work just for a boy . . ."

Kristin shook her head impatiently. "That isn't it. It isn't Bruce, Dad. It's just—" She broke off. How could she explain that sometimes she wanted to erase that "lifetime of work"—to do away with all the pressure?

"Kristin, sweetheart," Dorrie said soothingly, "you have to remember that the will to win is yours and yours alone. Neither your father nor I can give you that. If you feel we've been pressuring you . . ." She let her voice trail off, so it sounded almost like a question.

Kristin gulped. "I do feel that way sometimes. I feel I can't make any of my own decisions. I know I want to play tennis and I want to win, but I want it to come from me, you know what I mean?"

Mr. Thompson looked at her blankly. "We've tried to support you because you told us this was what you wanted, Kristin. Do you really think you're being fair?" Mr. Thompson cleared his throat. "Anyway, I don't see why any of us is getting so upset about this. After all, you did win the match today, Kristin."

Kristin stared down at her plate.

"And the way I see it, the most important thing between now and Sunday is for you to relax," he added encouragingly. "Try to take some of the pressure off yourself. Do what you can to get some of the joy back into your game."

Kristin felt a sudden flash of hope. Maybe he would understand about the party after all! "I'm so glad you feel that way," she said warmly. "I've been torn about whether or not to go to a party I've been invited to, and just before dinner I called to say I could come. I'm glad you won't be upset."

Mr. Thompson glanced quickly at Dorrie, then back at his daughter. "When's the party?" he asked her.

"Saturday," Kristin said, pretending to concentrate on her food. She didn't add, "Saturday *night*." But she didn't have to. She could tell how upset her father was from his silence.

Dorrie put her hand restrainingly on his arm. "You know," she said quietly, "I think Kristin is right about something. We've both been doing a lot of pushing for a long time now. Kristin's sixteen. If she makes the pro team, she'll be doing a lot of international traveling. She'll have some tough decisions to make, and we won't be there to help her." She gave Kristin a sad smile. "If we seem like we've been overinvolved, it's because we both love you so much, Kristin. We want what you want—or what we thought you wanted." She sighed. "In any case, I think it's important that you learn to make these choices on your own. If the party matters, fine. You're an athlete. You know your own limits and your own potential. The bottom line is, there's nothing anyone can do out there to make you win but you."

Kristin held her breath. Her father was quiet for what seemed like an eternity. "Dorrie's right," he said, looking at Kristin with sad eyes. "I'm sorry," he added gruffly, getting to his feet. "Sometimes I forget myself." And with that he walked out of the room.

Kristin felt her eyes fill with tears. "He means he forgets I'm not Mom," she whispered. And before Dorrie could say a word, Kristin pushed back her chair and dashed out of the room and up the stairs to her bedroom.

But even there, there was no escape. Tennis trophies glinted at her from the far corner, as if to say, "See? All those years and years of hard work, and you're suddenly deciding this isn't important!"

And there was the oval picture of her mother on the nightstand. This time when Kristin picked up the photograph, she thought her mother's eyes looked wistful, even through the laughter. It was as if she were saying, "Can't you do it for me, Kristie? Can't you pick up where I left off?"

Kristin sat still on the bed, holding her mother's photograph in her hands. Why was it after all this time of being so focused, of knowing exactly what she wanted to do and why, that she suddenly felt so lost?

It was like looking down a long dark tunnel, not knowing what she would find at the other end. The light she had seen there for so long wasn't there anymore to guide her.

Nine

Kristin had never been to a dance at the Sweet Valley Country Club before, and she felt uncomfortable walking through the front entrance alone. Bruce hadn't offered to pick her up—he had said he would see her there. Looking around, Kristin decided she had made a mistake in coming. Everything was so fancy! In the main room of the clubhouse, snowy linen tablecloths covered the tables, white flowers were everywhere, and little candles gave a soft-lit effect. To Kristin it looked like a movie set.

As guests started to fill the big room, Kristin realized her flowered sundress wasn't appropriate for the party. She looked down uncomfortably at her sandals, wishing she had called someone up to ask what to wear. The Patmans' guests were in formal attire, and the girls Bruce had invited from school wore filmy, diaphanous dresses. Some even had corsages, as if it were a prom. Kristin felt increasingly out of place.

Bruce was standing with his parents, greeting guests as they came in and steering people to the bar, where champagne and soft drinks were being served. "Kristin!" he said, walking toward her and smiling warmly. "I'm so glad you're here. I want to introduce you to my parents."

Just then Amy Sutton sailed up, looking like a model in her spectacular new dress. She had a gorgeous hand-crocheted shawl around her bare shoulders, and she practically threw herself at Bruce, ignoring Kristin completely. "I'm so sorry I'm late," she gushed. She turned to the Patmans with a welcoming smile. "What a lovely party," she cooed, tucking her arm through Bruce's as if he were her escort for the evening.

Kristin felt totally out of place. She waited for Bruce to break free from Amy and introduce her to his parents, but he seemed to be enjoying Amy's attention.

After a couple of minutes Kristin headed

toward the bar by herself. After all, Bruce was a host, she reminded herself. He had the rest of his guests to think about. He would come find her in a few minutes.

"Come here often?" Winston Egbert asked teasingly, joining her in the line for soft drinks.

Kristin turned to him with a grateful smile. She knew him from class and had always enjoyed his wisecracks. "To tell you the truth, no," she said. "Is there something I should know about how to behave?"

"Just don't take lessons from our hosts," Winston said wryly. "See that?" He inclined his head toward the place where Bruce was standing, with Amy snuggled beside him. "That's what happens when too much money, good looks, and ego all hit in the same place."

Kristin blushed. She had never heard anyone talk about Bruce before. Did he have a bad reputation?

She didn't have a chance to ask Winston more about his remark because Bruce was coming toward them, with Amy in tow. Kristin hoped Bruce was coming over to talk to her, but she turned out to be wrong. Bruce stopped to say hello to every single girl in the drink line. He flirted outrageously, asked several girls to dance, and passed Kristin by with a smile no different from the smile he had given everyone else.

Kristin bit her lip. Either she had been really confused about Bruce's invitation, or he had changed his mind, deciding she wasn't his date after all.

As the evening wore on, it became clear to Kristin that what Bruce wanted was to have his cake and eat it, too. He danced with her once, assuring her that he was thrilled she was there. He then had the nerve to say that having to spend time with anyone else was a complete bore, but the minute the dance was over he was off with Amy Sutton.

By nine o'clock Kristin was convinced she should never have come. She sank down in a chair to adjust the strap of her sandal. She was debating whether or not to leave when she caught sight of Elizabeth Wakefield and Jeffrey French.

"Kristin!" Elizabeth waved, hurrying over to join her. "Boy, I didn't expect to see you here tonight. Isn't tomorrow morning the final round of qualifying matches for the Avery Cup?"

Kristin nodded. "I'm leaving soon," she defended herself. What she didn't add was that she should never have come. It would have been one thing to jeopardize her match for a really special evening. But this was just one big waste of time.

"Well, good luck," Elizabeth said warmly.

"I'm sure you'll do well. Who are you playing against?"

Kristin frowned. "Sharon Owens," she said, trying to keep the nervousness out of her voice. "She's really good. It's going to be a tough match."

Elizabeth sensed that Kristin wanted to change the subject. "Some party, huh?" she said, shaking her head as she glanced around the ballroom.

Kristin nodded. "Yeah, it's some party," she said unenthusiastically. "But I think it's about time to call it an evening. I've got to get a good night's sleep if I'm going to be worth anything tomorrow."

She didn't bother trying to find Bruce to say good night. She thought he was probably dancing with Amy—again—and wouldn't even notice she had gone.

Her father had let her have his car that evening, and the minute she got into the car Kristin breathed a big sigh of relief and leaned back. She couldn't tell whether or not she was glad she had gone to the party. She'd had a horrible time and was very relieved to be out of the country club. On the other hand, it was nice to know she hadn't been missing anything! If this was what it meant to be normal, Kristin didn't want any part of it.

*   *   *

Sunday was one of the worst days Kristin had ever had. She felt she would never forget the match with Sharon Owens as long as she lived.

Kristin knew she wasn't well rested. When she got home from Bruce's party, she had been unable to fall asleep, constantly tossing and turning as images of the party flashed through her mind. She woke with a start at six in the morning, terrified she had overslept, and then she couldn't get back to sleep. By ten o'clock, match time, Kristin was all jittery. She played well in the first set and won fairly easily, 6–2. But in the second set everything fell apart. She served badly and her backhand was weak. She lost, 4–6. The third set was grueling. Both she and Sharon were playing with everything they had. After all, the girl who won would go on to play in the Avery Cup tournament, as a member of Nick Wylie's pro team. This last set was all that stood between Kristin and her lifelong dream.

Every muscle in Kristin's body ached with the effort of lobbing back Sharon's shots. The whole world seemed to vanish, except for the court and the ball flying back and forth between them. Sharon was ahead six games to five. Then they were tied, 6–6, which meant they would have to play a tiebreaker.

Both girls were beginning to get tired. The

score was nine points to eight, with Sharon still in the lead. A big crowd had gathered to watch, since the other matches were over. Nick Wylie, in his signature sunglasses, was watching from his usual perch in the bleachers.

It was Kristin's serve. The ball went into the net.

The spectators groaned in sympathy, but Kristin barely heard them. Her eyes were bleary, and she felt so tired she didn't think she could move. She took a deep breath to calm herself, but the second serve missed, too.

"Game and match," the umpire called out.

A huge burst of applause broke out, along with Sharon's delirious shout as she threw her racket in the air. Sharon had won. It was Sharon, and not Kristin, who had made the pro team.

Kristin wiped her face off with a towel, fighting back tears. She was so tired and depressed, she didn't think she would make it off the court without breaking down. But first she had to shake hands with Sharon and confront Nick Wylie.

"I'm sorry, Kristin," Nick said, coming onto the court and taking off his sunglasses. "You know we'll keep you as an alternate for the team. And you can always try again next year."

Kristin nodded blindly. An alternate. She couldn't believe it. After all she had worked for!

"Congratulations," she said stiffly to Sharon, trying to keep the misery from showing in her voice.

But Sharon knew how she felt. "I'm sorry, Kris," she said softly as they shook hands. All the competitors knew how much it cost to lose. And Kristin had lost more than a match that morning. She had lost the dream of an entire lifetime.

Dinner at the Thompsons' house was agony. Dorrie had joined Kristin and her dad, but no one had anything to say. They ate in deathly silence, broken only by short comments like "Please pass the bread."

Kristin couldn't eat a thing. She was wondering how she was going to break the news to little Emily.

"Can I be excused?" she asked finally.

Dorrie and her father exchanged looks. Mr. Thompson nodded, and Kristin felt as if her heart was breaking. She didn't have to look her father in the eye to know how much she had let him down. It was bad enough failing herself, but failing him was the worst thing imaginable.

Kristin threw herself facedown on her bed. She hated herself for having broken down during this tournament. To think she had wasted time going out with someone as shallow as Bruce Patman—that she had actually jeopardized today's match by going to his ridiculous party the night before! What was wrong with her? Didn't she have what it took to be a real athlete?

Kristin was so busy punishing herself that she barely realized the door had opened and Dorrie had crept in.

"Kris? Can we talk?" Dorrie said softly.

Kristin stared at her dumbly. "There isn't much to say, is there? I made a real mess of everything." She swallowed hard. "I don't blame you and Daddy for being ashamed."

"Oh, sweetheart, we're not ashamed! We're suffering because you're suffering!" Dorrie cried.

Kristin sat up woodenly and stared at her mother's picture. "I'm glad she didn't have to live to see what a failure I've become," she blurted out.

"Listen to me," Dorrie said firmly. "Your mother was a pro, Kris. She adored tennis. But there was something she loved a lot more than tennis, and that was you. I'm going to tell you something now that I probably should have told you a long time ago. Your mother was planning to quit tennis right after Wimbledon so she could stay at home with you and your father. She wanted a normal life. She wanted to have time to watch her daughter grow up." Dorrie blinked back tears. "She never ended up getting the chance, but I know if she were alive today she'd take you in her arms and say that being a winner in life doesn't depend on one match, or even a dozen matches. And you are a winner, Kristin Thompson. Do you hear me?"

Dorrie pulled Kristin into her arms, and for once Kristin's self-control shattered. She cried her heart out, sobbing as though she would never stop. Something hard and icy in her was finally melting. When she looked up, her face was stained with tears. "I miss her!" Kristin cried. She had always thought her mother was the perfect champion. But knowing that her mother had worried about making sacrifices made her seem more human—and it made Kristin miss her even more.

Dorrie was crying, too. "So do I," she said. And she hugged Kristin.

Ten

Kristin could barely face her father the next morning at breakfast.

"Good morning, sweetheart," Mr. Thompson said, looking up from his newspaper. "Did you get some sleep?"

Kristin felt worse than ever. The nicer her father acted, the more certain she was that he was just trying to cover what he really felt: profound disappointment.

Kristin poured herself a bowl of cereal, then said flatly, "I slept OK." She pushed the cereal away, her appetite gone. "Listen, I'm going to school. I want to get a head start on my homework before first period." She couldn't meet his gaze. "I'll see you this afternoon at the club, OK?"

"Kristin—" Mr. Thompson began, but she was already hurrying out of the room.

Kristin's heart sank when she saw Bruce Patman hanging out in front of the school with Adam Tyner and a few other seniors. Bruce was the last person she wanted to run into! She tried to walk past without stopping to say hello, but Bruce stepped in front of her, making little tsk-tsk motions with his finger.

"Now, wait a minute," he scolded her with a knowing little smile. "Just where do you think you're going? Aren't you even going to explain where you ran off to on Saturday night? I felt like a total jerk. I was just about to dance with you when—"

Kristin looked coldly at him. "Listen, I've got a lot of stuff to do," she said, trying hard to keep her self-control. She couldn't believe she had ever found Bruce Patman interesting. Now that she knew him a little better, she could tell how incredibly arrogant he was. The cocksure way he was grinning at her right now made her angry!

Boy, she thought, *I really lost my head for a*

while there. I sure hope next time—if there is a next time—I show a little bit better taste!

She started to push past Bruce, but he put a restraining hand on her arm. "You're not going to walk off without an explanation, are you?" he demanded hotly.

"Look, Bruce," Kristin said, pulling her arm away from his touch. "I don't owe you anything, least of all an explanation. In case you don't remember, you didn't pay one bit of attention to me the whole evening. And I happened to have had a match—a very important match—the following morning. If you worried about anyone even half as much as you worry about yourself, you would have remembered that." Without another word she stomped off into the building, leaving Bruce staring after her with his mouth hanging open.

Kristin slammed her locker shut several minutes later. It had been strangely satisfying telling Bruce off. He acted as if she was the first girl who had ever criticized him! Well, if that was true, she hoped she had started a much-needed trend. It might not make up for losing the match, but Kristin felt good telling Bruce what she thought of him. She felt even better knowing that what had seemed like conflict—between her rigorously disciplined tennis life and her sudden desire to lead a normal life—

hadn't really been a conflict at all. She had been flattered by Bruce's attention, but the truth was, she hated everything Bruce stood for. He seemed spoiled and immature to her. How could she have dreamed that anyone like him could ever interfere with her desire to play tennis?

Of course, the truth about Bruce's character had come too late. Kristin had lost her chance to be on Nick Wylie's pro team. Yet Kristin reminded herself that one loss didn't mean the end of everything. With a little hard work she could make a comeback—maybe.

In the afternoon Kristin headed over to Sweet Valley Grammar School. She had promised to meet Emily and take her out for an ice-cream cone, but she found herself dragging her feet. What would it be like, seeing Emily now that she had lost the chance to be on Nick Wylie's team? Would Emily still want to spend time with her?

To her surprise she found Emily sitting out on the steps by herself. Her face was stained with tears.

"Hey, what's the matter Emily, what's wrong?" Kristin asked anxiously.

Emily's lower lip quivered. "I'm not ready to

tell you yet. Can I just sit here for a minute before I do?"

Kristin nodded. "Of course!" she exclaimed. She felt ashamed of herself then for being worried about Emily's reaction to her loss. Obviously Emily had problems of her own.

Emily rubbed her eyes, trying to hide the fact that she was actually dashing away tears. "Something awful happened," she said miserably. "But I don't want to tell you because if I do, you won't want to be my big sister anymore."

"Emily!" Kristin cried, putting her arms around the child and hugging her tightly. "I'll always want to be your big sister, no matter what." She could feel Emily trembling as the tears began to come. "You don't have to tell me if you don't want to. But don't think that anything you say will change how I feel about you."

Emily sighed forlornly. "OK. But it's pretty awful." Her eyes were big and fearful as she studied Kristin. "I sent away for all this stuff so I could go to tennis camp. Yesterday I had the tryout, and I didn't make it." She covered her face with her hands, shuddering with mortification. "It was awful, Kris! I did everything wrong. I even knew it was wrong while I was doing it, and it still didn't help."

"Oh, Emily," Kristin cried, still holding her tightly. "And you really think that I wouldn't want to be your big sister anymore just because you didn't get into the tennis camp?"

"It isn't *just*," Emily protested. "I wanted to get in so badly, Kristin. If I had, I could have worked really hard to get better. But how can I without getting into the camp?"

Kristin nodded slowly. "I understand how disappointed you must feel, Emily. But I want you to know that what I feel about you has nothing whatsoever to do with whether or not you're a great tennis player. Get it?" She hugged Emily tightly. "I happen to be nuts about you," she whispered, "and not because you like tennis, but because you're you."

Emily slumped against her with relief. "I can't believe it," she whispered. "I was sure you'd hate me!"

Kristin was about to chastise Emily for being so silly when a bell went off in her head. Wasn't that exactly what she had believed her father and Dorrie felt about her? That they were ashamed of her because she had lost the match? That they would only love her as long as she kept winning?

She swallowed hard as she realized she had been every bit as crazy as little Emily. More crazy even, since she had known Dorrie and her father all her life.

Of course they loved her. Her, Kristin, for

what she was—and not because she won trophies or matches. Sure, they suffered when she lost, the same way she suffered. But tennis had been Kristin's choice, not theirs. She had been confusing their support and affection for pressure.

"You know, Emily," she said slowly, "I guess maybe you weren't so crazy after all. I think I understand why you feel the way you do."

"You do?" Emily asked, round-eyed.

Kristin nodded. "But the thing is, you have to find a way to separate what you want from what you think everyone else wants for you. It isn't easy, Emily. And I can guarantee it won't get easier. Whether it's tennis or something else you devote yourself to, you're going to put all your heart and soul into it—because you're like me, you're that kind of person. Sometimes—when you lose, especially—you'll hate yourself. And you'll think everyone around you hates you, too. But they won't."

Emily stared at her. "I know you lost yesterday. But it doesn't seem to bother you. You're such a champ, Kristin. Why can't I be like you?"

Kristin took a deep breath. She remembered what Dorrie had told her about her mother. "You can't idealize me, Emily. When I've won, it's because I've worked hard. Now I know I've got to work like crazy to get my game back, and that's what I'm going to do! I'm going to work as hard as I possibly can so I'll be in shape for the next crack at the pro team." She tousled Emily's hair. "In the meantime, I'm going to be helping you, too. I happen to think, with a lot of work, you'll get into tennis camp next year. You may have tried out just a little too soon."

"You really think so?" Emily cried.

Kristin nodded. "I really think so. But I also think that it's only going to work if you really improve your game. So you and I can work out together. How does that sound?"

Emily's eyes were shining. "It sounds great, Kristin!" She looked shy all of a sudden. "I'm so lucky," she whispered. "Nobody else has a big sister half as good as you are."

Kristin had to blink back tears. There were so many things she couldn't tell Emily. And one of them was that Emily had taught Kristin far more than Kristin had taught her.

For the first time she clearly saw that she had impaired her own tennis game by confusing love with success. She was going to have to learn the lesson that she had tried to spell out for Emily.

The most important thing for Kristin now— even more important than sticking to her schedule or working out more strenuously—was making the decision, once and for all, that competitive tennis was what she wanted.

Kristin had inherited her mother's love of the game, and love of competition, but the choices were Kristin's now, and she was making them for herself—not for her father, not even for her mother, only for her.

Kristin had idealized her mother the same way little Emily had been idealizing Kristin. She had never dreamed that her mother had had doubts about tennis. Now Kristin realized that everyone had doubts. Part of life was recognizing those doubts and learning to cope with them.

Kristin knew she would never again lose her concentration the way she had this past week. Too bad, she thought with a sudden pang, that the realization had come too late to be of any use!

Eleven

Kristin reread the essay she had just finished for Mr. Collins. "Not bad," she said to herself. She had actually enjoyed trying to define the American dream.

Once Mr. Collins had finished collecting the essays in class, he made an announcement. "You all know who the Samaritans are, don't you?"

Several blank faces gave Mr. Collins his answer.

"Well, the Samaritans are a group of business people who get together on a weekly basis for social and professional reasons. They sponsor a number of civic activities, some of them charity-oriented, like the annual picnic for impaired children, which some of you have been to.''

Kristin had heard of the Samaritans because they occasionally subsidized events before tournaments. But she wondered what they could have to do with English class.

''The Samaritans are sponsoring a community-wide essay contest,'' Mr. Collins continued. ''The topic is 'Sweet Valley in the Year Two Thousand.'

''You can write whatever you like, as long as you think it fits the title, and your essay should be no longer than five pages. The due date is in two weeks. I wanted to give you plenty of warning.''

''What do you get if you win?'' A.J. asked, looking interested.

Mr. Collins glanced down at the brochure he had been reading from. ''The first-prize winner will receive a one-hundred-dollar gift certificate at Laughton's, the bookstore downtown, as well as a medal of honor. The winner will also be crowned king or queen of the Citizens' Day Ball, a month from this Friday.''

A.J. grinned. ''I could go for that,'' he said. ''I wouldn't mind being king of the Citizens' Day Ball!''

Kristin smiled. Her own powers of expression had been challenged enough by the American dream essay. In fact, she was looking forward to having more time to practice these next few weeks. Today was Thursday, and though only a few days had passed since her disastrous match Sunday morning, she could already feel her game improving.

"Thanks, Kristin," Mr. Collins said to her when the bell rang and everyone filed out of the room. He nodded at her essay, lying on the top of the file. "I'm looking forward to reading this."

Kristin blushed. She wondered if he would guess how much of herself she had put into the essay. "The American dream is different for each one of us," she had started off. "But what every dream shares is a dedication to an ideal and a willingness to make sacrifices." She had gone on to describe some of the decisions she herself had been wrestling with over the past few weeks before analyzing the theme of the American dream in the novels they had been reading. She thought she had done a good job using a personal preface to the essay, showing how the novels had helped her to see the importance of hanging on to a dream.

"I hope you like it," she said shyly.

In the hallway Kristin ran into Elizabeth. "Kristin," Elizabeth said with a smile, "I was hoping to catch up with you today. Enid and I are going to have a big ice-cream party next week for all the girls participating in the Big Sister program, and their little sisters, too. Do you think you and Emily can make it?"

Kristin was about to remind Elizabeth that she had tennis practice every afternoon. Then she pictured Emily, and she stopped short. "When would it be?" she asked cautiously.

"We were hoping to do it Wednesday afternoon," Elizabeth said. "I know you usually have practice. Maybe you and Emily could come for just a little while."

Kristin nodded. "That might work out. She's been coming to the club with me almost every day now, to work on her tennis game." She grinned. "I guess it wouldn't hurt either of us to have some ice cream first and meet the other girls in the program!"

Elizabeth gave her a big smile. "Great. I'll count you in, then."

Kristin nodded. "By the way, Elizabeth, I want to thank you for getting me involved in the program. If you hadn't asked me, I never would have volunteered in a million years. And I'm really fond of Emily."

Elizabeth's eyes were very bright. "I may have been the one to invite you to participate, Kristin, but you were the one who agreed to do it. I can only imagine what kind of impact you're having on her!" She patted Kristin on the arm.

"It takes an awfully big heart to be able to give freely when you're as busy as you are."

Kristin just smiled. She was thinking how funny it was the way things turned out. A week ago she had been a nervous wreck. And now that the worst thing imaginable had happened—losing the chance to play in the Avery Cup tournament—she didn't feel devastated at all! She felt perfectly in control. For the first time in her life, Kristin knew what she wanted, and why.

She was going to work incredibly hard at her game, and when she got to try out again next year, she was going to show Nick Wylie what kind of tennis player she really was.

"Darn," Mr. Thompson said when the telephone rang that evening during dinner. Dorrie was over, and Kristin had helped make lamb chops. "I wonder who that could be?" He got up and answered the phone.

Kristin was so engrossed in listening to an anecdote Dorrie was telling that she didn't notice her father's eyebrows shoot up. "Just a minute," he said. "I'll put her on the phone."

He covered the receiver with his hand. "Kristin, it's Nick Wylie," he said in a low voice. "I think you'd better pick it up in the other room. It sounds important."

Kristin frowned. Just hearing Nick's name made her mouth go dry, and her heart started to pound. What could he possibly want?

"Hello?" she said into the telephone in the living room.

"Kristin, it's Nick Wylie," he said, his voice brisk and professional as always. "Listen, I've got a problem here, and I need to talk something over with you. Sharon Owens sprained her ankle today during her second match of the tournament."

"Oh, no," Kristin cried. "Poor Sharon!" She could only imagine the agony the girl must be feeling. To have fought so hard to get on the team only to get injured!

"Naturally she's very upset," Nick continued. "We all are. But the fact is, she won't be able to play in the tournament—or play at all for at least six weeks. She's seen the team doctor, and he's adamant that she stay completely off her ankle for at least a month, probably two."

Kristin twisted the telephone cord between her fingers, barely daring to hope what he would say next.

"Naturally we're all very disappointed for her. But we need to take steps to replace her on the team right away." Nick cleared his throat. "You're the first person on the reserve team,

Kristin. Would you be interested in taking Sharon's spot?"

Kristin could hardly believe her ears. "Yes," she said, fighting to restrain herself. "Yes, I'd be very interested." She took a deep breath. "How will it work? Do I just play until Sharon's ankle is healed?"

"Well, my plan was to let you fill in for Sharon at first and see how you play," Nick said. "To be honest with you, I was shocked that you didn't win on Sunday. It may well have been a freak thing. If your game stays strong, I don't see why you can't remain a permanent alternate on the team after Sharon's healed. As soon as a spot opens up, you could move off the alternate list. But," he added warningly, "that all depends on how your game holds up."

Kristin was so excited she didn't think she could contain herself. "When will my first match be?" she managed to ask him.

"Well, that's the problem," Nick said with a sigh. "Sharon was scheduled to play on Sunday, which gives you just a couple of days to get ready. And it's going to be a really tough match. Your opponent is a girl named Rachel Rose, and to be honest with you, she's going to be difficult to beat. She's been dynamite so far in the tournament." He paused for a moment. "You can back out if you want, Kristin. I can understand if you feel you'd rather wait and try again next year."

Kristin cleared her throat. "I'd like to play now," she said simply.

Nick laughed. "Attagirl!" he exclaimed. "OK, we'll need to get you out to Longview first thing tomorrow to start practicing." Longview was the club near Sweet Valley where the tournament was being held. "Do you think you can arrange to get the day off from school?"

Kristin assured him she could. When she hung up the phone she was in such a daze, she didn't think she'd be able to figure out what to do first.

"Honey, tell us what happened!" her father was calling from the kitchen.

All of a sudden the enormity of it all hit Kristin, and she dashed to the kitchen to engulf her father and Dorrie in a hug. "I'm playing! I'm in the tournament!" she cried, dancing around them in joyous circles.

She could hardly believe how excited she was. And she could hardly wait to call Emily to share the wonderful news.

Twelve

Late Friday afternoon Elizabeth and Enid were over at Enid's house, going through the list of girls who were participating in the Big Sister program. They were checking off the names of those who were definitely coming to the ice-cream party the following week.

"Have you called Kristin yet?" Enid asked, biting the end of her pencil.

"I spoke to Kristin in school. She said she and Emily would both come for a little while. Maybe we should call Emily to make sure, though."

Enid nodded and dialed Emily Brown's number. After three rings the girl picked up the phone.

"Emily? It's Enid Rollins calling. We're setting up a big sister–little sister ice-cream party next week, and we want to know if you can come," Enid said.

Emily sounded incredibly excited. "Oh, I'd love that," she said. "Only I don't know if Kristin can. She's playing in the Avery Tournament," she added proudly.

"She's what?" Enid said, her eyebrows shooting up. "But—I thought she lost her match on Sunday!"

"She did," Emily confirmed. "But Sharon Owens sprained her ankle, so Kris is taking her place. She's playing her first match this Sunday," she added importantly, "and I get to go and watch her! And guess what? I just know she's going to win! She'd been working really hard on her game. And she's been helping me with my tennis, too!"

"That's great," Enid said, starting to laugh. "Boy, I never thought I'd hear so much good news when I called you, Emily! Listen, when you get a chance, talk over the ice-cream party with Kristin and let us know whether or not you can come. If Kristin's free, you're both welcome, and if she's not, you can always come by yourself."

"Kristin's the best big sister in the whole world," Emily said loyally.

Enid smiled, her eyes softening. "It sounds that way," she said warmly. "It sounds like you're a great little sister, too. Hope to see you next week, Emily!"

"Kristin's in the Avery Cup?" Elizabeth demanded the minute Enid hung up the phone. "I can't believe it!" She jumped to her feet. "Enid, we've got to find out when her match is and get a big support group out there to cheer for her."

Enid nodded excitedly. "Let's call Longview and find out the schedule of matches for the weekend. Emily said Kristin's playing on Sunday," she added, starting to dial.

Elizabeth started to stuff her things into her backpack. She couldn't believe Kristin had managed to be part of the tournament after all. Everyone at school had been so disappointed when they learned she had lost her final qualifying match. In fact, Elizabeth was infuriated when she'd overheard Bruce telling some of his friends that Kristin really wasn't that good after all. "She doesn't have the spirit of a real champ," he had said dismissively.

As if Bruce knew what made a real champ, Elizabeth thought now. Well, Kristin would show

119

him. Elizabeth and Enid were going to do their very best to make sure to round up a huge group of fans to watch Kristin's comeback!

"OK, Kristin," Nick Wylie said, crossing his arms and looking at her thoughtfully. "I guess this is the moment when I'm supposed to give you a huge pep talk, right?" He shook his head. "But all I can tell you is that you've got a tough match in front of you. Rachel Rose has won every single one of her games so far in the Avery Cup."

Kristin took a deep breath. "You're not calming me down," she admitted ruefully.

It was Sunday morning, and Kristin was getting ready for her tournament match. Already the stands were packed with people. It was going to be a new sensation for Kristin, playing in a tournament this size. If only her first match wasn't against someone as aggressive as Rachel Rose!

"I'm only saying all this so you won't be too hard on yourself if you lose," Nick said, patting her on the arm. "I just want you to give it your best shot, Kris."

Kristin barely heard Nick's last words. She was watching Rachel pacing back and forth along the baseline of the far court, stretching out her arms and talking to herself. Rachel was a small, wiry girl with dark, frizzy hair and an intense expression. Kristin steeled herself. Then she smiled at Nick. "You know," she said softly, "I'm going to beat her, Nick."

Nick stared at her.

Kristin didn't say anything more. She picked up her racket and walked out onto the court, still smiling. She had never felt this way before. All of a sudden she radiated confidence, as though there was nothing in the whole world that could stand in her way. She waved to her father in the stands, and to Emily and Dorrie, who were sitting next to him.

"Go, Kristin!" She heard a roar and turned to see Elizabeth Wakefield. Kristin's eyes widened as she realized a whole crowd from school was in the stands. Her eyes picked out Elizabeth and her little sister Kim, Jessica, Jeffrey, A.J., Enid, Winston, Amy Sutton, Bruce. Bruce! she thought. What on earth was he doing there?

Well, she'd show him, she thought, tightening her grip on the racket. Kristin was determined she was going to play tennis like she had never played before. She had never felt as ready in her whole life as she did when Rachel came forward to serve.

The next few hours were the most intense Kristin had ever experienced. As Nick had predicted, Rachel was a powerhouse. Her serve was extremely strong for a young woman, and it took Kristin several games before she could return it without great effort. Rachel was fast, too. She darted from one side of the court to the other with lightning speed, lobbing the ball into a far corner or sending it slamming to the end of the court. Kristin ran harder and farther in the first set than she could ever remember. But she was keeping up. She lost the first set, 4–6, but she had proven to herself that she could keep up with Rachel. And she'd gotten used to her serve and her style. Now all she had to do was surpass her.

During the break between the first and second set, Kristin gulped down a glass of water and ran a towel over her face. As she thought about the next set, she told herself, "I'm going to beat her if it kills me!"

And that was exactly what Kristin did. She played the next set with a kind of concentration and energy that she didn't know she was capable of. She returned every single shot with speed and grace, and she kept Rachel running so much that the girl couldn't catch her breath. By the middle of the second set Kristin found out something about Rachel Rose. She was strong and quick, but she didn't have a backhand. Once Kristin found out her weak point, she didn't let her off. She kept whizzing balls to Rachel's left side, and Rachel began to lose. Kristin took the second set, 6–2.

The crowd was absolutely delirious. Everyone was cheering and crying out, "Kristin! Kristin!", barely able to believe that she had come from the position of underdog to tie the top-seeded Rachel Rose. But she'd done it. Winning the set made her feel extremely strong and refreshed. From the first game of the third set Kristin knew she had Rachel exactly where she wanted her. The dark-haired girl was exhausted, and Kristin just kept slamming the ball to her backhand. She won the final set six games to four, and the crowd went crazy.

"I can't believe it!" Nick cried, running out onto the court and throwing his arms around her.

The next minute Kristin was surrounded. Her father, Dorrie, Nick, Emily, a crowd of reporters, kids from school—everyone was jumping up and down around her. An official was presenting her with flowers, and Dorrie, tears running down her face, was trying to snap photos. Kristin felt as if she were in a dream. Rachel seemed to float toward her in slow motion, then reached out to shake Kristin's hand.

"I've never played a match like that," Rachel said slowly, shaking her head. "It hurts to say this, but you really deserved to win. That was an incredible match, Kristin."

"Kris!" she heard a little voice exclaiming.

She looked down to see Emily Brown, looking slightly shy and confused by the excited throng, reaching out her tiny hand to shake.

Then Kristin got a big lump in her throat. "Come here," she gasped and scooped the child up in her arms. She hugged her so hard that Emily cried out. But Kristin didn't want to ever let her go. She felt so full of joy right then, she thought her heart would break. She had everything in the world that mattered.

"Kristin," Mr. Thompson said that evening, putting his arm around her as they strolled into the restaurant where he was taking her to celebrate. "I'm really glad we're getting a chance to have dinner alone, just the two of us. I feel like there're an awful lot of things we need to talk through."

Kristin nodded. "I haven't been very easy to live with lately," she admitted.

"Well, I don't think I've been the world's most sympathetic father. Sometimes I get so excited by your success that I end up putting pressure on you without really intending to."

Kristin nodded seriously. "I'm glad we're going to have a chance to talk, too. There are some things I've been thinking about, and I really want to ask your advice."

Soon the two were seated at a window table and had ordered dinner, leaving them free to talk.

"You've been upset with me for weeks, haven't you?" her father began. "I get the feeling that you see me as something I'm really not. Like you think all I care about is whether you've won another trophy." His eyes were very serious. "Kristin," he said in an emotional voice, "would you believe me if I were to tell you that if you quit tennis today I wouldn't care? That all I want is for you to be happy?"

"I would believe it," Kristin said softly. "You know, before I met Emily, I don't think I would have. But now I think I have a little more sense of what it's like to love someone—to be responsible for them. I was disappointed when Emily didn't get into tennis camp, for her sake. But I didn't love her any less because of it. I was just sorry because she'd worked hard for something she wanted.''

Mr. Thompson nodded seriously. "I know you're going to have some very big decisions to make in the coming years. You know, you're growing up now. You're going to date—"

Kristin couldn't help interrupting. "You know, Dad, you were absolutely right about Bruce. He turned out to be the most arrogant, shallow, uncaring—"

Mr. Thompson put his hand up to stop her. "That may be, but I still wasn't right. I don't know Bruce. The truth was, I was trying to control your life. And that isn't my place. You were right, Kristin, and I was wrong. You're the only one who can learn to juggle all the different things you want. And it won't just be social life, either. You're going to have a lot of tough decisions to make now that you're a pro.''

Kristin took a sip of water. *Now that you're a pro.* Those words sounded like magic to her! Her eyes softened as she looked at her father. "I just hope I can always talk them through with you," she murmured.

Her father covered her hand with his, his eyes incredibly tender. "I hope so, too, Kristin.

Now there's something big I want to talk to you about. And I want you to tell me what you think."

Kristin nodded at him expectantly, but something deep inside told her that she knew what he was going to say before he began.

"It's about Dorrie and you, isn't it?" she said.

Her father stared at her. Then he started to laugh. "How did you know?" he demanded.

Kristin laughed, too. Actually, she didn't realize she knew until that very minute. But she didn't need her father to say one word more to guess that he and Dorrie were in love.

"Nothing's going to change for any of us," her father said slowly, "but Dorrie and I have been such close friends for so many years, and sometimes I find myself hoping . . ." He couldn't finish the sentence, and Kristin felt incredibly moved. She could only guess how lonesome her father must have been since her mother's death.

"I hope the same thing," she said, smiling at him. The look of surprise and relief on his face made her almost want to cry. It was so wonderful that they could finally talk to each other like this. Kristin thought then that for the first time in her life she was seeing her father as a person, not as someone to please or to disappoint.

"Now, let's have a toast," her father said,

grinning at her. He chimed his wineglass against her glass of water. "To the very best daughter a man could possibly have. And to the start of an amazing career as a pro player!"

Kristin grinned back at him, lifting her glass. "To love," she said. "To finding out it matters more than anything else ever could!"

Thirteen

Kristin was at her school locker Monday morning when she heard someone calling her name. It was hard to tell at first where the voice was coming from, and then she saw Bruce hurrying toward her with a distressed look on his face.

"Kristin, listen to me," he said before she could say a single word. "You were great yesterday—absolutely awesome. I'm not kidding."

"Thanks," Kristin said, opening her locker and trying to hide a smile. Bruce was so transparent. Now that she had won her match and was on the pro team, he would probably want to ask her out again!

Bruce seemed to relax a little when he saw she wasn't acting angry with him. "So," he said, leaning back against the locker next to hers and looking at her with a little smile on his face, "what do you think about letting me take you out to celebrate? I know this fantastic new Japanese restaurant downtown we could try, or—"

"Bruce," Kristin said, taking out the books she needed and turning to face him squarely, "now that I'm playing in the tournament, I'm amazingly busy. The fact is, I have to do everything I can to make sure I have enough time for family—and special friends." She looked at him significantly. "So you can understand why I have to say no." She started to walk away, and Bruce looked stricken.

"But, Kristin—" he cried, hurrying after her.

Kristin shook her head at him. "Just for the record," she said lightly, "you ought to try getting serious about something. It might be a nice change." And with that she started off down the hall, feeling a secret flash of triumph.

Despite her bad experience with Bruce, Kristin had to admit she had learned something from him. One day—maybe not too far away now—there would be someone special, and she was going to have to learn to make adjustments in her life so there would be room. But it had to be the right boy. And Kristin was more than willing to wait.

The ice-cream party for the big and little sisters was held Wednesday afternoon in the gym. A good number of people had turned out: all the girls participating in the program, as well as friends and several faculty members from school. Mr. Collins was helping Elizabeth spoon out healthy portions of ice cream for the make-your-own-sundae line, and Elizabeth's own little sister, Kim Edgars, was keeping her entertained with funny stories from school.

"Boy, it must be so cool getting to go watch Kristin play in tournaments," Allison Post said to Emily, big-eyed as she watched Kristin help the two of them to ice cream.

Jessica gave her little sister a funny look. "Allison," she said, "haven't we had a good time, going to the beach and the mall together?"

A.J., who had just come up from behind them to overhear this question, couldn't help laughing. "Uh-oh," he said. "Don't tell me we're getting competitive here!"

Jessica looked hurt as she watched Allison

scamper off to put toppings on her ice cream. "What an ungrateful child," she complained. "Here I've been doing all sorts of wonderful things for her, and she acts like she'd rather have Kristin for a big sister."

A.J. put his arm around her. "Listen, speaking of competition," he said, "I've got a draft of my essay for the Samaritans' contest. Will you take a look at it later and tell me what you think?"

"Sure," Jessica said. Her blue-green eyes shone. "So, if you win this contest, that means you get to be king of the Citizens' Day Ball, right?"

"Right," A.J. said, smiling down at her.

Jessica's mind was working fast. "What do they do about a queen if a guy wins the competition? They can't have a king with no queen," she pointed out.

A.J. laughed. "I guess the king gets to pick the queen, and vice versa. Why?" he demanded, tickling her. "Anyone I know happen to be interested in being queen?"

Jessica put her chin in the air. "I wouldn't mind," she said airily.

The truth was, just then Jessica was feeling that she could use a little extra fuss and attention. It had been a long time since she had been the center of things. And being queen of the Citizens' Day Ball sounded like just the way to do it!

Will Jessica get to be queen of the Citizens' Day Ball? Find out in Sweet Valley High #54, TWO-BOY WEEKEND.

<u>Prices and availability subject to change without notice</u>

Buy them at your local bookstore or use this page to order.

- -

SWEET DREAMS are fresh, fun and exciting—alive with the flavor of the contemporary teen scene—the joy and doubt of first love. If you've missed any SWEET DREAMS titles, then you're missing out on your kind of stories, written about people like you!

☐ 26789	PAST PERFECT #134 Fran Michaels	$2.50
☐ 26902	GEARED FOR ROMANCE #135 Shan Finney	$2.50
☐ 26903	STAND BY FOR LOVE #136 Carol MacBain	$2.50
☐ 26948	ROCKY ROMANCE #137 Sharon Dennis Wyeth	$2.50
☐ 26949	HEART & SOUL #138 Janice Boies	$2.50
☐ 27005	THE RIGHT COMBINATION #139 Jannah Beecham	$2.50
☐ 27061	LOVE DETOUR #140 Stefanie Curtis	$2.50
☐ 27062	WINTER DREAMS #141 Barbara Conklin	$2.50
☐ 27124	LIFEGUARD SUMMER #142 Jill Jarnow	$2.50
☐ 27125	CRAZY FOR YOU #143 Jahnna Beecham	$2.50
☐ 27174	PRICELESS LOVE #144 Laurie Lykken	$2.50
☐ 27175	THIS TIME FOR REAL #145 Susan Gorman	$2.50
☐ 27228	GIFTS FROM THE HEART #146 Joanne Simbal	$2.50
☐ 27229	TRUST IN LOVE #147 Shan Finney	$2.50
☐ 27275	RIDDLES OF LOVE #148 Judy Baer	$2.50
☐ 27276	PRACTICE MAKES PERFECT #149 Jahnna Beecham	$2.50
☐ 27357	SUMMER SECRETS #150 Susan Blake	$2.50
☐ 27358	FORTUNES OF LOVE #151 Mary Schultz	$2.50
☐ 27413	CROSS-COUNTRY MATCH #152 Ann Richards	$2.50
☐ 27475	THE PERFECT CATCH #153 Laurie Lykken	$2.50

<u>Prices and availability subject to change without notice.</u>

- -

MURDER AND MYSTERY
STRIKES

America's favorite teen series
has a hot new line
of
Super Thrillers!

It's super excitement, super suspense, and super thrills as Jessica and Elizabeth Wakefield put on their detective caps in the new SWEET VALLEY HIGH SUPER THRILLERS! Follow these two sleuths as they witness a murder . . . find themselves running from the mob . . . and uncover the dark secrets of a mysterious woman. SWEET VALLEY HIGH SUPER THRILLERS are guaranteed to keep you on the edge of your seat!

YOU'LL WANT TO READ THEM ALL!

☐ #1: DOUBLE JEOPARDY   26905-4/$2.95
☐ #2: ON THE RUN   27230-6/$2.95
☐ #3: NO PLACE TO HIDE   27554-2/$2.95

- -